AGGRAVATED ASSAULT

Chuck heard a screech. It was barely in time to alert him as someone leaped over the top of the shelves, slamming into him and knocking him to the ground.

But he immediately twisted and managed to hurl the attacker off himself. And there was more than just providing a defense this time. Chuck was moving with quickness and confidence that he hadn't been feeling earlier.

He put a hand out and stopped the assailant in his tracks without touching him. It was a teenager, all right, his face bizarrely painted, his hair looking as if it had been cut with a weed whacker. He shrieked in frustration and trembled, waving his fists around and demanding to be released.

"You can struggle all you want," said Chuck archly. "But you're not going anywhere unless I decide to let you go."

PSI-MAN

D0813701

PSI-MAN

HAVEN

Peter David

ACE BOOKS, NEW YORK

PSI-MAN: HAVEN

An Ace Book / published by arrangement with
the author

PRINTING HISTORY
Diamond edition / 1992
Ace mass-market edition / September 2000

The Penguin Putnam Inc. World Wide Web site address is
http://www.penguinputnam.com

Check out the ACE Science Fiction & Fantasy newsletter
and much more on the Internet at Club PPI!

ISBN: 0-441-00764-3

ACE®
Ace Books are published
by The Berkley Publishing Group,
a division of Penguin Putnam Inc.,
375 Hudson Street, New York, New York 10014.
ACE and the ''A'' design are trademarks
belonging to Penguin Putnam Inc.

PRINTED IN THE UNITED STATES OF AMERICA

10 9 8 7 6 5 4 3 2 1

Early Summer, 2022

1

The bulletproof tires of the RAC 3000 screeched around the curbside as the driver who wasn't driving screamed at the car to go faster.

Alex Romanova was leaning out the back window, firing at the three sleek black cars that were pursuing her through the early-morning streets of New York. Once upon a time, the screeching, screaming, and blasting high-speed caravan might have been enough to prompt *somebody* to call the police. But that was a very, very long time ago, when at least a handful of people still gave a damn. Also, that was when there were still police.

"Faster, dammit!" shouted Alex. "Faster! They're getting closer!"

"I am very aware of their proximity, Alexandra," replied the RAC 3000 primly in that female voice that Alex had come to loathe during their lengthy association. "I hardly think that profanity is an absolute necessity in this situation, do you? Oh, my finish!"

That last comment was in response to the spray of

bullets that ricocheted off her right rear bumper.

In response the RAC 3000, her gleaming red exterior marred but not terminally damaged, squealed around a sharp right turn, her engines throbbing with power. The instant that it did, she released a billowing cloud of fog that enveloped the dirty, rat-infested street of downtown Manhattan. The aesthetic advantage was that the eyesore avenue was no longer visible to passersby, had there been any. The strategic advantage was that the black sedan in the lead smashed headlong into a lamppost. The airbag cushion that inflated on impact saved the driver, but the gunner hanging out the passenger side was hurled straight out of the window. The good news was that his projectilelike fall was cushioned by a huge mound of uncollected garbage. The bad news was that his projectilelike fall was cushioned by a huge mound of uncollected garbage. He sustained numerous cuts and bruises that were minor in and of themselves, but they promptly became infected by the loathsome rubbish and he was hospitalized for two weeks.

Unaware of the fate of one of her pursuers—and, admittedly, uncaring had she known—Alex continued firing on the two cars that remained in pursuit.

The computerized mind of the RAC 3000, Ultraflame model, quickly scanned the map of Manhattan, charting the method of escape that would serve as the most likely to lose their pursuers while, at the same time, would be the most economical in terms of gas mileage. She also swerved slightly as her sensors detected more incoming fire, causing a bullet to just barely miss parting the short-cropped hair on Alex's head.

The RAC turned sharply again, this time onto Broadway, and barreled downtown. The two pursuing cars, for which the RAC had nothing but disdain (since they were what she referred to as "no brain" autos), followed. From within the cars there could be heard a loud and angry string of fluent profanity in Russian.

Alex took careful aim, fired again, and watched more of her ammo bounce harmlessly off the windshield of her pursuers. She likewise muttered a quick Russian curse, and fired again. This time the hammer clicked harmlessly.

She ejected the spent ammo clip, allowing it to clatter away on the street that whizzed underneath, and yanked another out from the pocket on her thigh. But just as she was about to slam the replacement clip in, the car made a small but abrupt swerve. She shrieked as the clip flew out of her hand and fell to the street. In seconds it was left far behind.

She slid back into the car with such fury that she thudded her forehead against the doorframe. "Goddammit!" she shouted. "You made me lose my last ammo clip!"

"There was a pothole," the RAC informed her icily.

"A pothole! *Jesus!*"

"It could have damaged my suspension system," was the calm reply. "Also you could have gotten a nasty crack, Alexandra. Would you care to hear some chamber music?" And before Alex could say no, music flooded the interior of the car.

Bullets thudded around them, *cracking* off the exterior, as the RAC 3000 hurtled through Cooper Union Square and angled down toward the Bowery.

"We're going to die," said Alex tonelessly. "After staying one step ahead of my former bosses for six months—six goddamned months—I'm going to die in the goddamned Bowery section of New York City, accompanied by a prissy car and goddamned chamber music."

"Your profanity is really getting a bit out of control, don't you think?" asked Rac.

And then something else hit the car . . . something that made a very different sound from the bullets. It was a sort of metallic sound, metal on metal, something that seemed as if it had affixed itself to the car's shell.

"What was that?" demanded Alex. "That noise . . ."

"We've acquired some sort of electronic device," the RAC told her. The car's electronic voice never wavered, but just for a moment it sounded vaguely apprehensive. "Adhering via a magnetic . . ."

And that was when the car went out of control.

It took Alex barely a second to realize that the RAC 3000 was no longer in charge of its forward motion. The light display that flickered whenever the car's voice spoke simply ceased. Even more bizarrely, after six months with the car and developing—dare she say it?—a rapport, she could simply sense that somehow the car's personality had just died.

In that time, Alex leaped from the passenger seat into the driver's seat and gripped the wheel firmly. But, to her horror, the steering wheel was locked. Immediately she realized what the problem was. "Rac!" she shouted. "Return control to me! Now!" for the guidance systems were still locked into computer control, except the computer wasn't controlling it.

And now the lights came back up and for just a moment Alex's hopes flickered up as well. That was until the car began to sing, very softly, "Daisy, Daisy, give me your answer true . . ."

"Shit," muttered Alex.

Whatever they'd attached to the car had done one hell of a good job.

Some sort of minilauncher had affixed a device that had scrambled all of the RAC's circuits. The engine was still going—the car was still moving—but there was no way to control it. As the old saying went, the lights were on, but no one was at home.

Alex put all her muscle power into trying to turn the wheel, but it was useless. She might as well have been a mosquito trying to knock a planet out of orbit: Definitely an "A" for effort, but don't expect fantastic results.

With no options left to her, Alex slammed on the brakes. Fortunately, those still worked. Unfortunately, there wasn't a great deal of time left for them to do their job. The car shot across the Bowery and smashed straight into a burned-out building on the other side.

However, the outer hide of the RAC was too tough to crumble under the impact. Instead, the car ricocheted like a pinball. Alex, who had had the good sense to strap herself in, screamed once as the car flipped clean over once, twice, and a third time before coming to rest a block away. Except it didn't come to rest—the car, flat on its roof, continued to roar as if in frustration, wheels spinning impotently.

Inside, the car's voice was cheerfully performing a lilting rendition of "On Top of Old Smokey."

Not wanting to wait around for the next chorus—since she was sure it was going to be a chorus of gunfire—Alex unstrapped herself, shoved open the door, and tumbled into the street.

As she did so, the two black sedans roared around the corner and started toward her.

She kept her gun leveled as she raced toward a nearby alleyway, looking over her shoulder with as menacing a glare as she could summon. Pure bluff, of course. But that was all she had.

She could see arms and legs sticking out from the shadows of the alley before her. The homeless and derelicts of which there were so many in the streets of New York. And bodies—lots of bodies. A population that was probably going to be increasing by one in the very near future.

A bullet whizzed just past her head, like an angry mosquito. Obviously they weren't too choked up about the possibility that she might fire at them. Then again, she couldn't say she was surprised. If she were them, she'd be feeling pretty confident about now, too.

She made her way through the shadows, stepping quickly and lightly over the assortment of projecting legs. There were moans and muttered growls from all around her. The voices of men and women, and the whimpers of a few children, protesting over their homes (homes!) being disturbed by this intruder.

Well, if they weren't thrilled about this, they were really going to hate it when there were more gunshots in just a moment or so.

And then there was a man blocking her way.

She could barely make him out, except to see the thick beard stubble that lined the lower half of his face, the upper half being obscured by a low-slung hat. It was hard to make out his form beneath his coat, but it appeared to be powerfully built.

He growled something at her, and a blast of alcohol

hit her in the face. "Get the hell out of my way," she snarled, and shoved him hard. She was a relatively small woman, but her muscles were like coiled springs, and he stumbled and fell backward into a heap of rubbish. Which was where, she reasoned, he belonged.

But the slight altercation had cost her precious minutes, and now she ran again, the entire time feeling that she was only prolonging the inevitable. Sooner or later she was going to be brought down. Sooner or later a couple of bullets were going to incapacitate her so that she could be dragged back to her homeland and infuriated bosses, or else a hail of bullets would simply save Russia time and trouble by turning her into Swiss cheese and leaving her lifeless body in the alleyway with the rest of the garbage.

If, however, it was to be a choice between sooner or later, she was going to opt for later if she could at all help it.

She stumbled once as she heard voices shout in rough Russian, "This way! She's down here!" and then she kept on going. All the while she kept saying to herself, in desperate, rushed whispers, "Don't let it be a dead end. Don't let it be a dead end."

Naturally it was a dead end.

The wall of another building faced her in stony, mocking silence. There was no place for her to go.

She spun and faced her assailants who, realizing that they had her trapped, slowed their pace. Within moments they were standing there, half a dozen of them, facing her from several yards away. Her back was against the wall, her gun out and pointed straight at the one in the middle.

"That you, Gregori?" she asked, squinting in the bare

light. The sun—the last one she would ever see, she figured—was just coming up over the horizon line.

He spread his hands wide in a most chipper fashion. "None but the best for you, Alex," he told her.

"I'd hate to have to kill you," she told him.

"A regret we would both share, Alex," was his even reply. "More so, I would think, since it would do you no good whatsoever. You're not going to escape from here, Alex. What good would it possibly do to kill me? That would accomplish nothing."

"It would make me feel a hell of a lot better."

Another voice, impatient—it sounded like Krakoff to her—said, "What are you playing at? Let's just kill her and get it done."

"You have an appointment, Krakoff?" she asked. "Better plans?" His sullen silence confirmed his identity to her. "Gregori, listen," she continued, trying to sound urgent but not desperate. Never show weakness. "We're on the same side, you and I."

"I would have to disagree. You're on that side, and I'm on this side. I don't see a tremendous amount of overlap," he informed her.

"What I did in San Francisco—it was for the good of everyone."

"What you did in San Francisco was act in direct opposition to your mission," said Gregori reasonably. "You had been given the mission to bring in Matthew Olivetti. Instead you took it upon yourself to kill him."

"He was dangerous. Uncontrollable. I was there and you weren't."

"Yes, that's true. Because if I had been there, then the job would have been done as it was instructed to be done. Korsakov was not happy with what you did. Not happy in the least."

"I gathered that," said Alex dryly. "He doesn't generally send a hit squad pursuing someone across a continent as a token of appreciation for a job well done. Gregori—you must believe me. Olivetti could have, would have, destroyed everything."

"I believe that you believe it," replied Gregori. "More than that . . ." He spread a hand and did not sound unsympathetic. "I truly am sorry about this, Alex. I genuinely like you. I really do. But you see I have no choice here. None at all."

And that was when the derelict—the one who had momentarily blocked Alex's path—stumbled forward once more.

He didn't seem to be paying any attention to the danger of the situation. Indeed, he might not even have noticed it at all. Instead he was staring intently at Alex, and then slowly started to point a finger at her. In a very distant voice, he said, "You . . ."

"Out of the way, idiot," said Gregori impatiently. He didn't like this business one bit, and the last thing he needed to do was prolong it thanks to the intervention of some bum.

For all the reaction it got, Gregori might not have said anything at all. Again the bum spoke, this time scratching at his beard stubble with his other hand. "You," he repeated, and this time there was the slightest tinge of recognition in his voice.

Alex's eyes opened wide. When the voice had been uncertain and halting, it was unrecognizable. But now, all of a sudden, there was just the slightest hint . . . the barest possibility . . .

He was on his way to New York, she thought dazedly, *but I was sure he'd have moved on by now. I . . .*

Gregori chose that moment to get physical. "I said," he informed the bum with uncontained frustration, "get out of the way!"

He grabbed the bum by the forearm.

That was a mistake.

The bum turned so quickly that in the dimness of the alleyway Gregori never even saw it. Had the same move been made in the middle of a street at high noon, it would probably not have helped.

All Gregori knew was that one moment he was endeavoring to shove the bum out of the way, and the next he was stumbling forward, carried that way by the force of his own motion combined with a very quick and decisive movement by the bum. The bum had simply gripped Gregori's forearm, turned with the thrust of Gregori's gesture while, at the same time, adding impetus from his own hip pivot.

The result was that Gregori hurtled through the air a mere instant after attempting to manhandle the bum, and smashed headlong into the nearest wall. He moaned and sank downward, clutching at his head and uttering a string of Russian profanity.

It had all happened with phenomenal swiftness. Yet there were still five armed men facing down the unarmed (save for an empty pistol) Alex Romanova, and a bum who had—in the opinion of Krakoff who was now charging forward—simply gotten lucky.

Krakoff did not share Gregori's softheartedness. For that matter, he was also one of the top agents when it came to hand-to-hand combat. He could have just shot the bum, of course, but he was going to take this opportunity to show Gregori up gleefully. And then he was going to make damned sure to let their superiors know that field head Gregori had not only been hesitant to dispatch the traitorous Romanova, but now he was unable to incapacitate a simple drunken street derelict.

He lashed out with a side snap kick, designed to catch the bum in the pit of his stomach. Once he knocked the wind out of him, he would then grab the bum by the shoulders, drive a knee up into his chin, put him down for the count, and then laugh in Gregori's face.

It was a simple and elegant, if somewhat vindictive, plan, and it worked flawlessly up until the moment that Krakoff actually tried to execute it.

The bum raised his arms straight up and turned on his heel just as Krakoff had committed to the first move. The result was that Krakoff's leg shot left past his target who had, gazellelike, sidestepped him. For a bare instant Krakoff's leg was fully extended, and at the same time, the power of the thrust was expended without having made contact with anything.

It was while he was in this off-balance position that the bum brought both his arms down and then up, shoving Krakoff's extended leg straight up. Krakoff felt a muscle pull in his groin and he screamed in pain and shock. Looking like a crucified ballet dancer, he was in no position to defend himself as the bum's right leg swept out, knocking Krakoff completely off his feet.

The Russian agent hit the ground and curled into a semifetal position, moaning loudly.

Now there were four.

Those remaining four, confused and alarmed, now aimed their weapons directly at the bum. He stood there, unmoving for a moment, and that was when Gregori had the supremely bad timing to stagger back from the wall that he had crashed into seconds before.

The result was that the agents couldn't start firing on the bum without hitting their field commander as well, something for which none of them was especially willing to assume responsibility.

The bum, for his part, wasted no time at all.

Moving with an incredibly fluid motion, he moved toward the remaining agents like liquid glass. They tried to surround him, but they never got the chance to complete the maneuver. The bum suddenly dropped to the ground, lashing out with one foot and tripping up one of the agents. The agent stumbled and fell against one of his partners and they both wound up tripping over the sleeping body of yet another derelict. The derelict barely paused in his snoring as the bodies of the two agents crashed down on top of him.

One of the remaining two agents swung a swift right at where the bum had been, but again he dodged, again he caught the arm, and this time spun completely around, slamming the agent into another one of his partners. They staggered for a moment, and the bum grabbed their heads in each of his powerful hands and slammed them together. It made a sound like two melons cracking, and they sunk to the floor of the alleyway without a sound.

The two who had fallen against the sleeping bum were trying to raise themselves up, and now Alex Romanova charged forward—stopping only briefly to give Krakoff a fierce kick in the head that knocked him cold. With expert precision, she delivered vicious chops to the base of their skulls that caused them to slump to the ground, unmoving.

She turned to face the bum and looked up at him wonderingly. "It's you, isn't it?" she said.

The bum looked at her uncomprehendingly. "I think I . . . know you from . . . somewhere . . ." His voice was halting, confused, as if all his confidence and quiet self-assurance had been ripped away. Was it indeed him? She wouldn't have thought it possible, but . . .

"Don't move."

The order had been barked by Gregori. Alex cursed herself for forgetting about him, even momentarily.

Now he was standing at the end of the alley, gun leveled at them, determination in his face. He was propping himself up with one hand against the wall, clearly trying not to pass out, staying conscious through sheer willpower.

"I really regret this, Alex . . . and whoever you are," he addressed the bum. "You are a wonderful fighter. I recognize the style. Aikido. But aikido can't stop a bullet."

His finger began to squeeze the trigger.

The bum reached out with his empty hand. It was a reflex effort. He didn't even seem to be fully aware that he was doing it.

And the next thing any of them knew, the gun was hurtling through the air, as if yanked by invisible strings.

It landed in the outstretched hand of the bum, who looked at it wonderingly.

Without hesitation, Alex grabbed it from his hand and aimed at Gregori. "I bet you regret things even more now, don't you, Gregori?" she asked with cold amusement.

He raised his hands slowly. "I think we can discuss this," he began.

Alex fired. The roar of the gun was deafening in the relative stillness of the predawn Bowery, and Gregori left his feet, his head snapping around. An incoherent *urkh* sound issued from his throat and then he collapsed like a puppet with severed strings.

She didn't even give him a second look as she began to gather up the guns she found scattered around the alley. The bum, for his part, stared at the unmoving body of the agent. "You killed him," he said tonelessly.

"No I didn't," was her brisk reply. Her denim jacket— hot as hell considering the summer months, but having the advantage of being rather concealing—was now bulging with the weapons she had gathered. It gave her a feeling of strength. Balance of power, that was what it was all about. In a way, she was almost tempted to stand there and wait for them to come around so that she could lord it over them for a bit. But that was beneath her, and a waste of time besides. "I just creased his skull. Even in this light, I'm a crack shot, Chuck."

"Chuck?" His voice sounded distant. "Chuck? I know that . . ."

"You're Chuck." She couldn't quite believe she was having this conversation. "Chuck Simon. The one the U.S. government calls the Psi-Man. The one my government, the Russian government, would love to get their hands on, just as much as your own would. Chuck. I'm Alex Romanova. You knew me also as Carmen Friedman. Don't you remember at all?"

He stared at her blankly. And then, in a confused voice, he said, "Could you buy me some coffee?"

"Do you know who you are?"

"I'm someone who wants some coffee." From his demeanor and his confusion, it seemed apparent that he was already oblivious to the men scattered about the alleyway. It was as if his synapses weren't working somehow. As if a fog had simply dropped down and settled onto his brain, preventing important information from getting through. Information like his name, and who he was, and what he could do, and why any number of intelligence agencies in the world either wanted him dead or working for them, or some happy combination of the two.

"Sure," she said. "I'll get you some coffee." She put a hand on his shoulder. "But first you have to help me."

"What do you need?"

She was surprised to find that her voice had acquired a singsong tone to it, as if she were addressing a child. "My car is upside down."

"It must be hard to drive it."

"Yes, well I don't like it that way and I was hoping to make it turn back right side up. I was hoping you could help me with that."

"How?"

Within moments she had dragged him back to where the car had overturned. She was amazed at the slowness with which he was moving. He was a trained athlete and aikido master, and yet now, away from the reflexive movements of battle, he acted as if he were walking underwater.

"See that car? Make it turn over."

"How?"

Again his voice had that sort of otherworldly distraction to it, as if he were addressing her from another planet. "Think about how you want it to be right side up. Remember? Like you wanted to get the gun to fly out of the man's hand before."

"Did I do that?" he asked.

Gods! Not only couldn't he remember the distant past, he had trouble with short-term memory!

What in hell had happened to him?!

She cast a nervous glance in the direction of the alleyway. Nothing was stirring from within, but she had no idea how long that was going to last. Of course, she had all the guns, but what if she had missed some? Or perhaps reinforcements could show up.

"Dammit!" she snarled and, striding quickly over to the car, started shoving at it with all her strength in hopes of rocking it back into the more accepted position for locomotion. A moment later, in an imitative fashion, the bum she had called Chuck was beside her, rocking as well.

He cast a grin at her in the sort of open manner of a child and then, with a thrust that was beyond anything that either of them was generating with their arms, the RAC 3000 suddenly flipped over. It landed with a thud on sturdy tires, started to tilt once more as if threatening to continue to turn over before settling in an upright position.

Fortunately enough the engine had shut down . . . perhaps some sort of automatic response to the car's having been incapacitated. Alex quickly scoured the exterior until she found the thing that had caused all the problems— an electronic device about the size of her fist, which had doubtlessly been fired by some sort of launcher. It had stuck to the car's hull with a high-powered magnetic base, and wreaked hell with the computer.

For one moment Alex feared that the damage had been irreparable, but the RAC 3000 was far too sophisticated to be terminally incapacitated. Within sixty seconds of having the electronic jamming device removed, the RAC 3000 had run a thorough systems check and was ready to roll.

Naturally the vehicle recognized its former owner immediately. "Charles!" said Rac in surprise. "It is good to see you again. And how nice . . . Rommel isn't with you. He shed all over my upholstery, you know."

Chuck looked at the car in surprise and then turned to Alex with uninhibited wonder. "It talks!" he said.

"Get in," said Alex tiredly. She practically shoved him into the passenger side, went around, and climbed into the driver side. "Get us out of here. Get us anywhere. Queens. That sounds good."

Obediently the RAC started up, and Alex looked at Chuck. He was gleefully looking at the RAC's light display, as if hypnotized by it.

What in God's name had happened to him? His power, his memory? And, for that matter, the RAC had brought up a good point.

Rommel was the massive German shepherd who had accompanied Chuck everywhere. The two had a link she couldn't even begin to understand. It seemed to border on—or perhaps even surpass—the telepathic. Chuck and Rommel actually seemed to speak to each other. They were inseparable.

So where in the hell was Rommel?

2

Sometime Earlier . . .

At first there was nothing.

Nothing except the sound of his own heartbeat, only it sounded very far away.

For the first time in what seemed a long time, he started to have a vague sense of himself. But he wasn't certain who that self was.

And then something else filtered through to him. He didn't know over what period of time those other things filtered through—days, months. Maybe he'd been here for millennia. Time was utterly irrelevant.

He decided to open his eyes.

The time from the moment of decision to the actual opening of his eyes seemed, to him, instantaneous. It was, in fact, three days.

When he did open them, he could barely see anything. There was some sort of thin gauze running directly across his face, diluting the glare of the overhead light. He heard no people nearby, although there was the slow, steady *beep* of some sort of life monitor. Now what in hell could it possibly be?

Where was he?

Who was . . .

How . . .

Recollection started to drift back to him. He remembered a face, hovering in front of him. Dodging him. Mocking him. He remembered chaos all around, and berserk cartoon characters. And a rocket.

God . . . that rocket . . .

At that moment he heard someone enter, with the soft sound of shoe leather scraping on the floor. He could tell by the momentary pause that whoever had entered was looking at the beeping machines. The monitors. His life signs were being monitored, that was most definitely the case.

He heard a remote, thoughtful "Hmmm." And now a face appeared, hovering over him, backlighted like an angel with the overhead lights giving a halo, corona effect. He couldn't make out much of her, but he was able to see her eyes looking down at him.

She took a closer look, peering through the gauze into his eyes. If she was startled or shocked to see someone looking back, she didn't indicate it. She merely called out, in a slightly raised voice, "Doctor! Doctor, the patient is awake."

Long moments (hours, days?) later there was a doctor next to her, also peering down. He frowned and said softly, "How long has he been awake?"

"I checked the monitors just an hour ago and there had been no change in the readings. But now when I looked, I saw there was a marginal increase. I verified it with a visual assessment of his physical status."

"You mean you looked at his face," said the doctor, who did not sound unamused.

"Yes, sir."

The doctor leaned a bit closer. He appeared to be in his late forties, early fifties. Bald on top but his graying hair was long on the sides, and appeared to be pulled back into some sort of ponytail or braid—it was hard to see from this angle. He was peering through tortoiseshell glasses, but removed them now as he studied the patient. "Mr. Beutel, do you hear me?"

Beutel tried to respond, but couldn't get his mouth to move.

"You may be having difficulty talking," said the doctor.

No fucking shit, Sherlock, Beutel thought. For some reason he found the mental profanity to be reassuring.

"We want to see if your cognitive abilities are functioning. I can see your eyes clearly. If you can hear me, please blink twice in rapid succession."

Instead of simply opening and closing his eyes, Beutel opened and shut first his left eye, and then his right. This drew a small smile from the doctor, who said, "All right, Mr. Beutel. It's clear you still have some degree of a sense of humor left. That's very fortunate, because after what you've been through, you're going to need it to sustain you. I'm Dr. Faber. Dr. Martin Faber."

The name rang a bell with Beutel, and the vague recognition in his eyes must have been apparent, because Faber nodded briefly. "That's right. I'm the expert in cybernetics who created the metal prosthetic that replaced your arm. That was handled by one of my students, Dr. Chabora, and was done quite well, I might add. But for the extent of the damage you've undergone, your superiors at the Complex felt that it would be best if I handled this personally. Do you remember the Complex?"

Beutel did nothing this time, waiting to see what Faber would fill in.

"The Complex?" prompted Faber. "The intelligence organization that you work for? Do you remember?"

Of course I remember, you goddamned moron, Beutel thought bleakly. *And I remember Simon . . .*

It all came back to him in a dizzying rush.

Chuck Simon and he, Reuel Beutel, the top psychic assassin of the formidable Complex, battling it out atop the great castle in the middle of Wonder World, the massive amusement park/armed camp of wealthy entertainment mogul Wyatt Wonder.

Beutel had had Simon cold. Had him dead to rights. Simon was reeling. But did Beutel use his psychic ability to try to finish Simon without laying a hand on him? Oh, no, hell no. He had wanted to crush him. Had wanted to pulp Simon's square-jawed, heroic face beneath the cybernetic muscles of the mechanical fist that had been at the end of Beutel's arm. The arm that had been destroyed by Simon's hellhound, Rommel. He had owed Simon for that, owed the damned dog as well. But first Simon was going to suffer, Simon was going to die . . .

But Simon had dodged, with that preternatural speed of his. It should have only been a temporary setback, as Beutel's metal fist and forearm sank deep into the gleaming wall of the tower that Simon had been standing in front of.

And then, to his horror, Beutel had been unable to extricate his fist. He had yanked. He had screamed. He had howled. And then the platform beneath him had started to shake as the metal tower revealed its true purpose—it was a missile, a goddamned rocket, headed for who knew where. And try as Beutel might, he couldn't yank his fist out. Some sort of bizarre sealant had held it fast, and when the rocket launched, leaving Wonder World far behind, it brought along with it a souvenir: the screaming form of Reuel Beutel.

The rocket had angled upward, upward, and Beutel had realized that its destination was space. Driven by panic and desperation, he had applied all of his formidable telekinetic power against the surface of the rocket, pushing away from it with everything he had. He focused all his psychic strength, and then he screamed as he tore away from the rocket, his sleeve flapping in the breeze as his prosthetic forearm was left behind.

Blood had fountained from the stump, but that had been the least of Beutel's problems. His main concern was that he was, at that moment, thousands of feet up and starting to plummet.

He had spread his arms—or rather, his arm and a half—and begun to manipulate the air currents as his power enabled him to do. He had managed to slow down his descent considerably—

But not stop it.

Like a meteoroid, he plunged to earth. His memory was hazy on where exactly he had landed, and perhaps his mind was trying to block it out. Sparing him the agonizing memory of what had happened.

All he knew was there had been a bone-crushing impact, and he had felt as if his body were exploding out of every pore. Then a haze of red, followed by a haze of black.

But surpassing everything, even the conviction that he

was shortly going to die, was the desire to kill Chuck Simon. It had rolled through him like a great, burning wave. Never had he so wanted someone to die as he did Simon.

"Reuel," Faber was saying softly, "the damage was very extensive. Do you remember falling?"

Beutel blinked twice, this time not even bothering with the smart-ass alternating eye blink.

"Fortunately for you, the Complex was able to track your trajectory and find you. But it took them two days. It's nothing short of miraculous that you're still alive."

It had been no miracle. Just good, honest hatred, and a fury too consuming to die.

"I have done everything that I can. You were in and out of surgery for three months. Frankly, we weren't sure if you were ever going to come around. That you did is a very pleasing sign."

With pure force of will, Beutel forced his lower jaw to move. When he spoke it was in a voice that was thick and gravelly and barely recognizable as his own. *"Get me . . . the fuck . . . out of here . . ."* was his low and almost animal growl.

The nurse appeared taken aback, but Faber merely nodded in approval. "Very good, Reuel," he said. "Keep that fire. Keep that anger. You're going to need that as well as any sense of humor. You're a fighter. That's what I like about you. That's what makes you such a perfect subject for the extreme measures I had to take in order to preserve your life. I hope you understand."

Beutel blinked twice, and eagerly looked forward to the moment when he felt strong enough to murder this oaf and get on with his life . . . and with the death of Chuck Simon.

And Simon's goddamned dog.

3

The store on Ocean Avenue had long been disputed
territory. That wasn't surprising—since it was a supermarket, the treasures it held were considerable. The meat
had long ago spoiled, of course, giving the entire supermarket the distinct air of a funeral parlor. It took a strong
stomach just to get up the nerve to get near the place.
But it was also a tremendous source for canned goods,
the sort that the people collectively known as the Forsaken had come to depend on.

Googie was one of the foremost foragers, and now
had taken it upon herself to try and stake a claim for the
Forsaken on that marvelous storehouse of canned goods.

She squatted down a moment opposite the supermarket, pausing to brush the stringy brown hair out of her
green eyes. Then her gaze narrowed as she saw a guard
step out of the market, glancing left and right to see if
anyone was in the vicinity.

She recognized the guard and his colors almost immediately. His blue and red jacket designated him as a
Pezzhead, as did the perpetually goofy expression on his

face. Pezzheads were so-called for their favorite drug, which they called their "candy" and generally sent their minds somewhere into the lower ionosphere. Whenever they would ingest this particular unauthorized substance, their heads would invariably snap up and down, up and down, like a particular kind of antique candy dispenser. Hence their group name.

But even in their fuzzed-out states they were still considerably dangerous, and Googie had to proceed with extreme caution.

She checked the cylinders on her weapon and nodded. Fully loaded, she had all the tranq barbs she needed to do the job. Occasionally she would get ribbed by some of the others—especially Figurine—about her reluctance to kill. But she saw no need to. Whereas the others seemed to feel that life was pointless and cheap because of the situation of the world, it was Googie's opinion that the current state of affairs only made life that much more precious.

The problem was that the lookout was out of range of her dart gun.

Furthermore, if he was out there, then it meant that there were others in the store. So even if she ditched the guard, she'd just be walking into who-knew-what.

She breathed an inward sigh of relief that she had her backup, her partner, Zorro, hiding somewhere nearby. Now where was he? She scanned the area but didn't see him. Well, she knew that he was in the vicinity. Blessed be the day that Brainpan had brought Zorro to them. He'd done it to impress Googie, of course. His infatuation for her was evident to all. This didn't make Googie feel any less flattered by it nor, for that matter, any less inclined to use it to her advantage whenever possible.

Well, thought Googie . . . here went nothing.

She had been crouched behind a row of garbage cans, but now she thrust out with her slim but powerful legs. The cans clattered over noisily, leaving her exposed to view.

The Pezzhead guard immediately snapped around and saw her. His face broke into a lopsided grin. It wasn't hard to see why—Googie, despite her general tendency to avoid bathing, was not unattractive. Furthermore she was dressed in cutoff jeans that showed off her formidable legs, and a flowered shirt that was tied off just under her small breasts, displaying a flat and firm midriff. The dart gun was in her right hand, but she made sure that that was still discreetly behind the one remaining garbage can.

Over one shoulder she was carrying a large satchel in which she was intending to bring her loot—provided that she was able to make it into the store.

The Pezzhead shouted, "Hey, guys! Look what we got here!"

Obediently, two more Pezzheads emerged from the supermarket. They wore on their faces the exact same goofed-out grin that the lookout was sporting.

They started toward her with swaggering confidence, making off-color suggestions and remarks, informing her of just what they were going to do with her and hell, she was going to enjoy it, wasn't she. And on and on until they were less than five yards away, at which point Googie brought her gun up into view.

The Pezzheads looked at one another, and grinned even wider. "Awwwww, cuuuuute," said the lookout.

He was the one that Googie shot first. He looked down in surprise at the dart that was lodged firmly in his shoulder. He tried to tug at it and muttered, "Bitchin'," before collapsing to the ground.

Googie's gun spat twice more before the remaining two Pezzheads could even realize that they were in trouble. Within seconds they had joined the lookout in the middle of Ocean Avenue, unconscious.

Googie didn't hesitate as she charged across the street toward the supermarket.

The leader of the Forsaken, the Magistrate—the most powerful and respected person she knew—liked to tell the Forsaken how once upon a time the streets of Coney Island had been bustling with life during this time of year. How automobiles had crowded the streets, and tourists had strolled the Boardwalk.

Not anymore, of course. Not since the Calamity.

Googie pushed thoughts of that bleak event—so recent, and yet seemingly an eternity ago—out of her mind as she entered the supermarket. As always, she managed to ignore the stench of the rotting meat. After all that she had been through and seen in her relatively short life—she was only twenty-two—a few unpleasant aromas were nothing.

She headed straight for the canned goods aisle, but just as she turned into it, a quickly moving form slammed into her.

She let out an alarmed shriek as one of two Pezzheads, who had apparently not joined their associates when the guard called them out, hurled her to the floor with such force that her dart gun skittered away across the floor. She rolled to her feet and screamed, *"Zorro!"* just as the larger of the Pezzheads grabbed her by the back of the head and slammed her down to the filthy floor.

The Pezzhead was a particularly vile specimen, with a series of obscene tattoos decorating his shaven head. Worse, he didn't seem to be under the influence of their preferred drug at the moment, which explained his unusually clear head and overall vicious demeanor. When Pezzheads were flying, no matter what they did to you they were pleasant about it. This guy wasn't flying, however.

He grinned down at her with rotting teeth and said, "You got a friend with you, bitch? That it? You got some son of a bitch covering your ass?"

"Oh, yes," said Googie in a strangled but unafraid voice. "A genuine son of a bitch. The biggest son of a bitch on the block."

An instant later, this was confirmed by the sounds of paws thudding across the floor of the supermarket, claws making a furious *klik-klak* sound as their owner charged toward the source of the call for help.

The Pezzhead looked up in confusion, and then he wasn't confused anymore. He was just terrified.

Skidding into view was a massive dog, a German shepherd. He was brown and black, with an odd "Z" shape in the fur of his forehead. Dangling from either side of his body were large, empty satchels, and they didn't look like they were going to slow him down at all.

When he growled it was like a truck that needed a muffler. When he roared—as he did now, upon seeing his partner on her back, her legs splayed—it was like sticking your face into a jet engine. He looked capable of swallowing an arm whole—which, on one occasion, he had.

"Shit!" screeched the bald Pezzhead. *"Shit!"* He

lunged, trying to go for Googie's gun, which was nearby.

He wasn't nearly fast enough. The dog that Googie had called Zorro charged across the remaining distance in no time flat, his jaws open wide. He intercepted the Pezzhead's lunge and his huge teeth clamped down on the Pezzhead's neck.

The other Pezzhead screamed as his friend's Pezzhead separated from his Pezzneck, rolling across the grimy floor and coming to rest at the screaming man's feet. The dead Pezzhead was staring up with a very surprised expression on his face. His mouth even moved slightly, although whether that was just some sort of after-death reflex action or a dying attempt to utter some sort of profound last word was impossible to say.

Either way, the remaining Pezzhead didn't want to stick around and find out. Instead, with a screech, he turned and bolted.

"Let him go, Zorro!" shouted Googie, but inwardly she knew it was no use, and she was right. Zorro leaped over her and landed full on the back of the fleeing Pezzhead. The screaming man rolled over and tried to pound on the side of the dog's head. This was a serious mistake . . .

Googie looked away, barely able to tolerate the screams, or the crunching and snapping noises that accompanied them. She certainly had no intention of looking at the actions that matched the sounds.

When the sounds of slaughter finally ceased, she turned and looked back at the mess on the floor. Zorro stood, forepaws foremost, in a small pile of gore and blood. "I certainly hope," she said tersely, "that you don't expect me to clean all this up."

Zorro looked at her blandly.

After a moment, Googie sighed in a "whattaya gonna do" type tone, went to Zorro, and briefly ruffled his fur. He bowed his head slightly in appreciation . . .

And then he raised his head.

"Zorro?"

He cocked his head slightly, as if sniffing the air. He actually seemed puzzled, as if he were expecting to find something but didn't know what. As if he had heard a voice . . .

"Zorro, are you okay?" asked Googie.

He turned his gaze on her and, for just a moment, saw someone else. And then it was gone.

But a word remained. No, not a word. A name. A name that sounded vaguely familiar.

Chuck?

4

No one knew for certain, or would ever know for certain, just who exactly had been responsible for blowing up Pittsburgh, or how they had done it.

The "why" part of the equation had not been difficult to discern. The president, who was frequently referred to simply as "The Man," was supposed to be in Pittsburgh on that day in January of 2022 when the explosion had occurred. It was generally assumed that the intention had been to obliterate the commander in chief of the most powerful military-industrial complex in the international arena known as the New World Order. No less than seventeen terrorist groups, including some that even the Complex had never heard of, claimed responsibility for the act.

The Complex had spent a great deal of time and energy tracking down each and every lead, and after all of that time and energy had been expended, the result was a considerable number of dead terrorists and obliterated terrorist organizations. But they had not been able to prove conclusively which of the groups was in fact behind it . . . or if any of them had been. The general theory now was that the Russians had been behind it, but they couldn't prove that either.

All they knew for certain was the following:

The president, miraculously, was safe. The reason was simple: He had not been in Pittsburgh at the time of the detonation. Instead the vice president had gone in his place, wearing a disguise that made him a dead ringer for the president so that he could impersonate the chief executive for the Pittsburgh appearance.

It was the vice president's responsibility to substitute for the president during all functions that the president could not or would not attend. In order to eliminate possible disappointment in those instances, the vice president frequently wore a clever and rather impenetrable disguise. Likewise his voice was indistinguishable from the genuine president's voice. This was not accidental.

It had been with these very kinds of instances in mind that the president had chosen as his running mate one of the most popular celebrity impersonators in the entertainment industry. The guy was capable of imitating practically anyone who was in the public eye, and he specialized in political figures. He had been the ideal campaign partner. He'd gone out on the road and, in his various personal appearances and holo-vid gigs, worked up such a deadly and devastating impression of the presidential opposition that it had made the opponent a laughingstock to much of the electorate. It had been so effective that the president was convincingly reelected; convincingly in that no one suspected that the election was pretty much a predetermined affair in the first place. Nowadays, elections were referred to in the upper echelons as "bouquets," because they were always very carefully arranged.

The other advantage to the elected vice president was that, with a wig and a fake nose, his imitation of the president himself was perfect. Too perfect, as it turned out.

It had been the vice president, delivering a speech to the Veterans of Out-of-Country Armed Persuasion Actions (formerly known as the Veterans of Foreign Wars), who had been blown to kingdom come by . . .

What?

Nobody was certain of that either.

Ground zero of the explosion had been determined to be the Ozone Reconstruction Plant just outside Pittsburgh. The problem was that that plant did require nuclear materials to be on premises. It was one of life's great ironies that the machines endeavoring to repair the atmosphere were powered by devices that Eco-terrorists (once called environmental activists) decried as being even more dangerous to the continued existence of life on earth than the loss of ozone.

The explosion, powered by the nuclear materials plus something else—something undetermined—had blown the plant sky-high just as the disguised vice president was twenty miles away. He was about to launch into a really good opening joke. Instead he, along with the entire audience, was launched into orbit.

No one was ever able to find any remains of the vice president, or the audience, or the device that must have caused the explosion . . .

Or Pittsburgh.

What was left instead was a crater, miles wide, miles deep. Smoke had poured out of it nonstop since the explosion, and it was shortly after the destruction that scientists had determined that the explosion had cut right down to the earth's magma layer. In other words, a mini-volcano had been created right there in Pennsylvania.

The impact on the already beleaguered environment had been devastating. The air had carried the ash and soot east, cutting a swath across Pennsylvania straight through to New York. Hundreds of miles were declared an ecological disaster area. The government began a salvage operation, but there was only so much they could do.

To all the affected citizens, they gave the same advice: If you were ever considering moving out of New York—especially the five boroughs—now would be an excellent time. To add emphasis to it, they granted massive credit increases to anyone who opted to relocate.

Providing money for such things was not a problem these days. After all, money was—to all intents and purposes—eliminated. Instead all adults had personal credit accounts, to which the government could add at any time. Those accounts were accessed via the ubiquitous "Cards" issued at birth to all citizens.

By the same token, the government could take away (much like the Lord). And what they made clear that they were going to take away—in order to provide the credits for those people choosing to move—were various government-provided services such as garbage collection and police.

(The fact of the matter was that the president had been trying to shut down New York City for ages. It had been one of the few strongholds of active political opposition left in the country. Not only that, but he had seen a film many years previous, the old celluloid kind, called *Es-*

cape From New York, in which the whole city had been transformed into one huge jail encampment. That had always sounded like a pretty good idea to him, and it was a goal toward which he was actively working. While he wasn't thrilled about losing Pittsburgh, in his opinion it would be worth it if he could dispose of New York at the same time.)

Most of the population of the five boroughs, over the next months, had obediently emptied out, because that was the logical thing to do. Most major businesses had already relocated to more pleasing parts of the country than New York, and the ones that were left now took the option that had been provided to them through the combination of terrorism, environmental chaos, and governmental directive. Money was being provided. The president wanted it done. (And, hey, wasn't it damned lucky that he wasn't killed in that hideous business in Pittsburgh?) And so it was done.

But not everyone had moved.

There was a handful of very old people, of course. People who had lived their lives in New York and were too stubborn to go anywhere. The president had decided not to make a big deal about this. Not a lot of old people went out to vote these days anyway, and besides, they would die soon.

Then, of course, there were the types of people who could always be found feeding off decaying cities, in the same way that you could always find maggots, appearing as if from thin air, crawling over remains of rotting meat. They were the derelicts, the dispossessed, the forgotten, and the uncared about. The worms eating away at the Big Apple.

The true New Yorkers.

The last pioneers. The final frontiersmen, boldly going where everyone on the planet was going together:

Straight to hell.

5

Alex Romanova, formerly known as Carmen Friedman, had decided to make a pit stop in hell. What this meant was stopping in Queens.

Getting lodging these days was extremely easy in the New York City area. All one had to do was drive around and pick a house. The vast majority of them had For Sale signs stuck in front of them in a perfunctory manner. There really weren't buyers. The signs were there more out of habit than anything else.

Alex's eyes narrowed until she found a particularly nice Tudor house on 189th Street in Flushing. The For Sale sign had grown rusty, creaking slowly in the very light breeze like a saloon door in an Old West ghost town. The shutters were all closed, and the doors were locked with heavy-duty, absolutely infallible, pick-proof locks. They took Alex a little over two minutes to crack.

"Come on," she said firmly to Chuck. He nodded slightly in that vacant and distracted manner he had that was really getting on Alex's nerves. She had no idea what was going on with him, but she was going to have to do everything she could to find out as soon as possible.

The electricity was off, of course, and the entire house had a thick musty smell. There was no furniture, but there was a brown shag carpet that looked comfortable enough. Certainly Alex had stretched out on far worse.

She was also relieved to get the hell out of the RAC 3000. Despite the car's superior filtration system and the fact that the air conditioner had been going full blast, it had not been enough to relieve Alex of the oppressive aroma that was being generated by one Mr. Chuck Simon.

She prayed that the water was still turned on.

Chuck ran a finger across the dirt that had collected, apparently an inch thick, on the window. He turned and said hopefully, "Any food?"

"Yeah, I got food," said Alex. "In the car." Which she did. She had been very meticulous in stocking up as she went.

He nodded and headed toward the door. But Alex stopped him, placing a hand firmly against his chest. "Not so fast, Cochise." She nodded in the direction of the stairway that led up to the second floor. "Go upstairs, find a shower, and get cleaned off."

"All right," he said affably, and went upstairs.

She went out to the car and, as she got her supplies out of the rear, said to the RAC 3000, "Keep an eye out for any potential problems."

"I do not possess eyes," the RAC informed her. "Would it serve equally as well if I kept my sensory apparatus in a state of yellow alert?"

"Yeah, that would do just fine."

"Very well."

She went back into the house, firm in the knowledge that the RAC 3000 had the situation firmly in hand. Or tire. Or something.

The sound of a shower running upstairs was a source of blessed relief. She plopped down in the middle of the living room, spreading her various canned goods around her. The hot plate with which she cooked was fully powered up, having been charged off the RAC's batteries.

Before she started cooking, though, she pulled her large glasses out of her bag and put them on, to aid her vision in the darkened room. She also lit up a cigarette. Months ago she had quit. She had been so proud of herself. But with everything she had gone through since quitting, she felt she was doing herself no favors from further restraint. After all, the whole point of quitting smoking was to help you live longer. Since she was convinced that her life expectancy wasn't anything extraordinary, what was the goddamned point?

For what it was worth, she had also gone back to her chocolate obsession that she had bottled up years ago. She was on the run, with ten more pounds on her hips and a smoker's cough. And a ratty haircut. She ran her fingers absently through her hair and made a mental list: Keep the cough. Keep the weight. Lose the ugly haircut. There, she thought with great satisfaction as she took a drag, filling her lungs with noxious fumes. No one could accuse her of scrimping on self-improvement.

She opened a couple of cans of precooked ravioli to warm up on the hot plate. Above her the water ceased running. Chuck was finished with his attempts to rejoin the human race.

He trotted down the stairs and smiled amiably. When Alex looked up at him, her mouth thinned into unamused lines. "Don't you think you might want to consider putting on some clothes?" she asked.

He looked down at his nudity, as if noticing it for the first time—which perhaps he was. His hair, slicked down, was pale and hanging over his ears, half down to his shoulders. His beard stubble, thicker than before, had a few streaks of gray in it. Considering what he had been through, it wasn't at all surprising.

Except . . . he couldn't seem to recall what he had been through, could he.

A strong sense of priopriety prevented Alexandra from glancing lower—after an initial quick and reflexive and slightly guilty look—to see if the rest of his hair had any gray in it.

He looked at her, water still dripping from the ends of his hair, and said, "My clothes were all dirty. I didn't see any point in putting dirty clothes back on me if I was all clean."

It was hard to argue with logic like that. Blast, he looked good. The muscular, well-trained body held a lot of appeal to it. And damn, it had been such a long time since she had . . .

And he probably wouldn't remember it even if they . . .

She immediately dismissed the idea. Wouldn't be right. Wouldn't be proper. Fun, yes, but not right or proper.

"Go upstairs," she said firmly, "and see if you can find anything up there to put on. I'll check around downstairs."

She got up, pulled out a flashlight from her emergency pack, and went down into the basement. There she lucked out as she found two large cardboard boxes filled with old clothes. They were hopelessly worn at the knees and elbows, and obviously had been left behind on the assumption that somebody else would get around to carting them over to a goodwill box or something.

She gathered the most likely-looking pants and shirts together and brought them upstairs. There, Chuck was waiting for her and proudly displayed the one item that he had been able to scrounge upstairs—a beat-up pair of pink fuzzy slippers. One at a time, he held his feet up for inspection.

"Swell," said Alex unenthusiastically. "Here." She tossed the clothes to Chuck, and unabashedly he pulled some of them on. The pants were short at the cuffs by several inches, and the shirt was tight across the chest, but they were serviceable. He dropped down on the floor opposite her, looking at her with puppy-dog openness.

Easily the second most dangerous man she had ever met, and at the moment he seemed about as threatening as an artichoke.

She sat there and watched him chow down on the ravioli, and when he was done he looked like he was ready to eat the can.

"Okay, Chuck," she said softly. "Now that we got you washed up, and fed . . . we have to find out what in hell happened to you."

"Okay," he said, sounding just as calm and uncomprehending as he had earlier.

She scooted across the carpet on her butt until she was only a few inches away from him. She took his hands in hers, as if she felt that the only way to establish any sort of rapport was to be in physical contact with him. "Now you want to tell me how in hell you wound up in that alleyway?"

"Okay."

She waited for him to continue. She waited for what seemed an interminable amount of time.

"Well?!" she finally exploded.

"Well what?" He truly didn't seem to comprehend.

"Tell me!"

"I want to tell you," he said. He shrugged. "I just was. I've always been there. It's my home."

"No it's not."

"Where is my home?"

"It's . . ." She paused, and then shook her head. This was turning into one strange damned day. "Okay. Your home is in a town called LeQuier, Ohio. You haven't been there for close to two years, though. With me so far?"

He nodded. Whether he was genuinely following what she was saying or not was very difficult for her to tell. Gamely, though, she pressed on.

"You were a gym coach there. Your name was . . . well, it is, actually . . . Chuck Simon. You were living a quiet life, teaching school and also practicing a self-defense discipline called Tomiki aikido . . . notable in that it consists entirely of defensive moves and no offensive ones. Oh . . . and you're a Quaker. You stridently believe in nonviolence. Are you remembering any of this?"

He thought about it, and it was difficult for her to read what was going on behind those crisp blue eyes of his.

The next time he spoke, it was with a bit less of the vacuousness that had marked his earlier intonation. "When I stopped those men in the alley," he said, giving it a great deal of consideration, "it bothered me. They wanted to hurt you . . . and hurt me . . . but I didn't want to hurt them. It upset me to hurt them."

"Yeah," she said, nodding slowly. "Yeah, that sounds about right. A half-dozen bruisers try to perforate the two of us, and what upsets you is that you might hurt them. So here's what happened with you. A top intelligence organization in the country, the Complex, discovered that you have psychic abilities. You're a powerful TK, Chuck. You can maneuver objects using the strength of your mind alone." At his blank look, she said simply, "You can pick things up without touching them. You think about them going up into the air, and they do."

"Really?" He seemed very intrigued by the prospect, but displayed no inclination to try it out.

"So the Complex recruited you, to train you as a psychic assassin. And they teamed you up with a dog—a monster of a German shepherd you named Rommel. You can communicate with him telepathically. Without moving your mouth or anything."

"So I pick things up without touching, and talk to a dog without moving my lips." He sounded skeptical. She couldn't blame him. If she hadn't made a thorough study of the entire file, she would have had trouble believing it, too.

"That's right," she said evenly. "But when you discovered what they wanted you to do, you ran away, and took Rommel with you. Since then you've been on the run."

"And how come I know you?"

The last thing she wanted to do was describe for him, chapter and verse, their previous meetings. She had been less than honest with him—hell, had lied outright.

Double-crossed him, used him. Maybe his amnesia wasn't such a bad thing at that.

"I'm . . ." Again a long drag on a cigarette. He seemed unaware of the fact that she was deliberately taking a long time to try to put the best face on things. "I'm with another organization. A group that thinks the Complex shouldn't be allowed to do whatever they want. You and I met in San Francisco. While we were there, I had a bit of a falling out with my bosses, just as you did with the people who run the Complex. Now in your case, what they want to do is drag your ass back to their headquarters so that they can lobotomize you or something. Turn you into the perfect psychic assassin robot. Me, my bosses just want to blow me to kingdom come because we disagreed over how to handle a mission."

"They sound like tough bosses," he observed.

She nodded once, curtly. "They are at that," she agreed. "Now that's the short version of your history and mine. Which still leaves my original question—how in hell did you wind up in that alley? What happened to Rommel?"

He stared for a long time into the empty can of ravioli, as if all the secrets of the universe were somehow hiding inside there. "I don't know," he said at last. "I feel like I should know him. Like I should remember him. Like I should remember you. Like I should remember this power you talk about."

"You used it. You used the power in the alleyway," she said, sounding somewhat exasperated. "Don't you remember?"

"I think I do. Everything happened very quickly. I don't know . . . all you've told me about sounds so strange and—it's as if you're talking about another person."

And that was when she grabbed a knife and lunged at him.

Even seated, on the floor and totally relaxed, his reaction was instantaneous. He swung one arm up and brushed aside her forearm before it even got close. A quick twist of his hand and he flipped Alex completely over.

She yanked away from him and kept rolling. "What are you doing!?" he shouted, but she had already gotten several feet away, and from a kneeling position, she hurled the knife.

It was not particularly dangerous. It was a butter knife. The most hazardous thing on it was the tomato sauce, which hadn't tasted particularly good. Nevertheless, it was a hurtling object, and it was coming straight at his face.

He stopped it. Without touching it.

He stared at it with a uniquely stupid expression, incredulous, and then he released it. It fell noiselessly to the shag rug.

Without a word, Alex held up a small candy bar. "Dessert?" she asked quietly.

"How . . . how did I do that? *Did* I do that?"

She took his lack of response to her question to be a lack of interest in the candy bar. This sat just fine with Alex; all the more candy bar for her. "Yeah, you did it," she said as she tore open the candy bar. "You and nobody else. So you see, whatever did this to you didn't drain off your abilities or anything. It just put you in a frame of mind wherein you can't recall your frame of mind. Follow?"

He shook his head miserably.

"I didn't think you would," she said amiably. "Don't worry, sport. We'll get it sorted out. I have a trick or two up my sleeve that might help. It helps that my schooling was in psychology."

"Why?"

Before she could answer, she heard the roar of motors in the distance. Several of them, and she could tell from the sound of them that they were motorcycle engines. Quickly she stood and crossed to the window, peering out through the slats of the shade. Across the street, the large cross that hung on the abandoned Catholic school had a dummy nailed to it, with ketchup dripping down to resemble blood dripping from stigmata. The words "In God We Trust" had been scribbled across the dummy.

"Cycle Sluts," said Alex after a moment.

Chuck walked over and stood next to her, looking tentatively through the shade. Now assembling next to the RAC 3000 were about half a dozen women, dressed in leathers, atop motorcycles that had been decorated with human skulls and other similarly cheery accoutrements. They were studying the RAC with tremendous fascination, chortling and laughing. The RAC, for her part, was making no move.

"Just some of the cheery inhabitants of Old New York," Alex told him in a low voice. "There're several female biker gangs around. They're not just part of the New York scene. They have chapters all over."

He watched them warily. "At least you don't have anything to fear from them."

She turned and looked at him with just the slightest touch of amusement. "I don't?"

"No. I mean . . . it's not like a gang of men. I mean, you'd have to worry that if they caught you, they might . . . well . . . rape you or something. But not them."

She uttered a brief laugh that sounded like a sort of bark. "Kiddo, that is exactly what I would have to be afraid of when it comes to them."

He looked at the bikers uncomprehendingly and then back at Alex.

She nodded curtly. "Dykes on Bikes. They're always looking for some new . . . members. So if it's all the same to you, I'd just as soon keep my voice down, okay? Besides, the RAC can handle this."

"Are you sure? I mean, it's just a car."

"It . . . *she* . . . was never just a car. And I've been doing some alterations on her during the past few months. I can be pretty handy with a set of power tools."

"I know. You talked about having a few tricks you could use."

"That's about ri—" Her voice trailed off for a moment and then she said, "Okay. This could start to get interesting."

Outside, the cyclists had gotten off their bikes and were circling the RAC 3000 appraisingly. Neither Chuck nor Alex could hear what was being said, but one of the women was now trying to pull open the door. This was being met with a singular lack of success. Angrily, she kicked the driver's side door.

"Oh, that was a major mistake," said Alex.

And barely had she gotten the observation out when the driver's side door flew open. It smashed into the assailant and knocked her flat. Then, before anyone could make any sort of response, the door slammed shut again.

"Very nice," said Alex coolly. Chuck merely looked on in amazement.

The leader of the group pulled herself up off the ground, rubbing her jaw in irritation. She walked around to the front of the RAC 3000 and proceeded to kick the right front fender.

"An even more major mistake," observed Alex.

Abruptly the mighty engine of the RAC 3000 roared to life, and before the group leader had time to realize what was happening, the RAC bolted forward with a screech of tires. The only thing that saved the woman was that Rac wasn't bothering to go at full speed.

The front of the car caught her up and flipped her onto the hood. She screeched and clung on as Rac turned sharply, ignoring the howls and shouts from the other members of the Cycle Sluts. With one hand the leader was holding on to the sideview mirror, and with the other she was pounding in utter futility on the windshield.

The car suddenly slammed to a halt, but the woman naturally kept going. She hurtled like a missile off the hood and crashed into a lamppost. Her remarkable toughness enabled her to stagger to her feet, but she wasn't able to do much more than that.

The RAC suddenly shifted gears and roared forward once more, straight at the woman with arrowlike precision. There were yells of alarm from the other women that gave her the split-instant's warning she needed, and she lunged desperately out of the way. The RAC crashed into the lamppost once more, and this time knocked the lamppost over. The tall object fell over like a great silver tree, its cry of twisting metal sounding like a death scream.

Utterly unharmed by the impact, the RAC 3000 spun about to face the women once more.

They backed up, looking at each other as if trying to see whether anyone else had a clue as to how to deal with this berserker vehicle.

Not remotely inclined to allow them to collect their scrambled wits, the RAC charged forward yet again. They scampered to avoid the car, and the RAC plowed into and over the motorcycle of the leader. It had been the biggest and most impressive of the lot, with streaks of black and silver painted on it. Now, however, it was a twisted hunk of scrap metal. The RAC did have to slow down as it finished passing over it, but that only took a moment. Then the RAC spun about, ready to charge again. The motor roared in defiance.

This was more than enough for the Cycle Sluts. They leaped onto their remaining motorcycles, the leader jumping on the back of one of them, and accompanied by the stench of burning rubber, the motorcycle gang peeled out.

The RAC seemed to watch them go for a long moment, and as the sounds of the cycle engines faded into the distance, the mighty car then very quietly, and very sedately, rolled back to its parking spot. The engine shut down and the RAC 3000 just sat there, unassuming. If it had not been for the twisted and destroyed motorcycle next to the curb, one would have had no inkling that anything unusual had happened a few moments ago.

Chuck turned speechlessly to Alex, and then managed to get out, "*Where* did you get that car?!"

"From you," said Alex calmly. This was all so strange for her. She was used to knowing more about people than they thought she knew, but knowing more about someone than they themselves knew, well . . . that was definitely an odd one. "It was a gift from a guy named Wyatt Wonder. What can I tell you, Chuck. You have some powerful friends." And then her face darkened and she added, "And some even more powerful enemies."

6

Quint stared up at the starship *Enterprise* using his one good eye.

As was his custom, Quint was wearing dark clothes, and a hat pulled down low. It wasn't for the purpose of avoiding attention drawn to himself. That wasn't a consideration at all. Quint's expertise was having people not notice that he was there. Indeed, as he gazed up at the model of the famed TV starship (back when there was TV), people walked past him and didn't even glance his way . . .

Except for one. A child, his mother leading him by the hand, slowed down as his mother pulled him through the Smithsonian Air and Space Museum. She was anxious to show him some other portion of mankind's accomplishments in the field of aviation, particularly the model of the space station that had been launched in 2011. But the little boy, for his part, was far more interested in the odd man that they were hurrying past.

"Mommy, is that man a pirate?" he asked in what

would have been called a stage whisper were it not a child speaking.

His mother didn't hear him at first, and then when she looked where he was pointing, she didn't seem quite able to focus on what he was pointing at. Then she blinked and shook her head slightly, and it was as if she were seeing the tall, darkly dressed man for the first time. Then she saw the reason for her child's inquiry—the black eyepatch that Quint sported over his right eye.

"Oh! I'm sorry," she said quickly to Quint.

He inclined his head slightly to indicate that no offense was taken. "It's an honest mistake," he said simply. "No, son. I'm not a pirate." And then in a slightly lower voice he said, "I'm a Secret Agent."

"Ooooooohhh," said the little boy.

The mother, who had had more than enough of this—already her face was coloring slightly from the embarrassment caused by her son pointing out Quint's physical handicap—hauled the child away without further discussion. Quint watched them go, his face impassive in stony-faced silence.

And then a low voice said next to him, "Most amusing."

He didn't even bother to turn as he said, "Hello, Genady."

"Greetings, Quint."

As if he had all the time in the world—as if he weren't in mortal danger merely by standing in the Smithsonian Institute in the company of the man who was next to him—Quint went back to studying the model. "Did you ever see that program?" he asked, nodding his head in the direction of the starship model.

"Which version?" replied the man called Genady.

"The original series? Or the *Next Generation*? Or the one after that . . . *Federation's Fall*?"

"Any of them."

"Oh, all the time," said Genady with a dismissive wave. "Charming novelties. Preaching a brotherhood of the future. Interesting fantasy, don't you think?"

Slowly Quint turned to face Genady Korsakov . . . the man whom several intelligence reports presently on Quint's desk swore had been killed at various times in the Ukraine, Japan, and Italy.

Genady was a surprisingly avuncular-looking man. Stone bald, with thick gray eyebrows that were a bit owlish, he was a few inches shorter than Quint, and when he spoke it was with a deep rasp—the result of a lifetime habit of smoking unfiltered Russian cigarettes. His eyes were set deep in his face, but they tended to crinkle at the edges in amusement, as if the entire world were some sort of tremendous joke and only he was in on the punchline. The odd combination gave him the curious appearance of being both friendly and dangerous at the same time.

"I happen to like fantasies," said Quint. "They provide the basis for much of human growth."

"I see," said Genady softly. "I see."

"Did you blow up Pittsburgh, Korsakov? You or your people?"

Genady Korsakov laughed silently at that for a brief moment. "You've been dying to ask me that in person, haven't you?"

"Did you do it?"

"No."

"Would you admit it if you had?"

"No." Korsakov was quite polite about it. "I'm afraid I wouldn't. Terribly sorry."

"No need to apologize. I understand."

Genady eyed him speculatively for a moment. "What if I told you I had? For the purpose of disposing of your president?"

Quint shrugged slightly. "I'd say you've got lousy aim and piss-poor intelligence capabilities. Considering that the president was in Colorado, you missed your target by several thousand miles."

"Yes, that was unfortunate." Genady blew irritated air from between his lips. "A great tragedy. All those innocent people. Not to mention the vice president who, may I say, when the mood was upon him, did an exceptional Judy Garland impression. Pity to lose a man like that due to a case of mistaken identity. There just aren't enough good entertainers in the world."

"That's show business," Quint said in commiseration.

Once again Quint was subjected to Korsakov's steady gaze. "You," said Korsakov, extending the word so that it seemed to be three syllables long, "youuuu would not have been especially upset had we been successful. Would you?"

Genady always noticed that with his people: When someone was saying something that they weren't supposed to, they always cast a glance around reflexively, in an endeavor to ascertain whether anyone or anything was watching or eavesdropping. To Quint's credit, however, he merely said what he wished to say without ascertaining their relative privacy. Yes, credit . . . or perhaps utter foolhardiness.

"The president—and his aide, Terwilliger—have been scrutinizing the Complex with excessive intensity

these days," said Quint after a moment. He spoke calmly
and evenly. Genady suspected that it took a great deal
to get any sort of rise out of Quint. The chances were
that even when he had lost his eye, his pulse had not
jumped much above the norm. "If the spotlight of their
attentions were to be shut off, I would hardly weep at
the prospect. But what's done is done, and what wasn't
done can only be regretted."

"You speak treason."

Quint shrugged. "As Errol Flynn once said in regards
to that same statement: 'Fluently.' Enough of my political leanings, Genady. It's time to move on."

"Indeed. Especially considering that you asked for this
meeting."

Quint looked at Genady with something resembling
mirth, or at least as close as his perpetually impassive
face ever allowed him to get. "*I* asked for it? I don't
recall contacting you."

"Quite true. Quite true." Genady smiled broadly, apparently quite self-satisfied. "Then again, with men such
as ourselves, direct intentions are not always necessary,
are they? I knew you would be here, and you knew that
if you came intending to meet with me, that I would be
here. We each of us act in accordance with our individual gifts, do we not, my dear Quint?"

"You offer some valid points," said Quint after a moment. "But from what I understand, several of your op-
eratives had difficulty recently acting in accordance with
their individual gifts, didn't they, Genady?"

Genady blinked in surprise. "Now, how," he demanded, not able to keep the amazement out of his
voice, "did you find out about that so fast?"

"We have our secrets that you are privy to, and you

have yours that we get in on. Our understanding is that your people ran into some trouble in New York last night."

"They're efficient to a fault with reporting in, it would seem, if someone in my organization got you the information that quickly," said Genady. It was clear from his tone that he was not simply going to let matters go, but instead plug the leak that had gotten the information out. Then he shrugged. "Why deny it? It's quite true, yes. One of my field squadrons was in pursuit of a runaway agent. She was involved in that paranormal business some months back in San Francisco."

"The Olivetti boy," said Quint with a nod.

Genady did not even consider doing Quint the insult of asking how he had come by his knowledge of Matt Olivetti. His head bobbed up and down, like those old statues people used to have in the windows of their cars, with the heads on a small spring. "Quite correct. She had been tracked down and brought to bay in Manhattan, where my field agents were planning to . . . inform her of our dissatisfaction."

"Inform her how? Planning to have her bite the bullet?"

"We were intending to terminate her employment," said Genady with excessive charm.

"And, not coincidentally, her."

"We do what we must."

"But not always. Not this time. You ran into problems."

Korsakov began to walk, his arms draped behind his back. Quint fell into step beside him. "A man," he said, "who dressed and spoke like some common derelict—

but hardly acted like one. He tore apart my trained team as if they were rank amateurs."

"How?"

"Hand-to-hand combat mostly, plus . . ."

His voice trailed off and Quint, thinking *In for a penny*, finished gamely, ". . . plus, he displayed telekinetic powers?"

Korsakov didn't even look startled that Quint knew. "Oh, yes. Displayed them quite prominently, I must say."

"Destroyed your team."

"Elapsed time of a little under sixty seconds, by the estimates of the team leader."

"Did he have a dog with him?"

Genady stopped and turned to face Quint, a befuddled eyebrow raised that accentuated his owlish appearance. "No. Then again, the alley was dark. If it was a small dog . . ."

"Oh, this would have been a big dog. And you know just how big a dog it would have been. And since we're talking dogs"—and Quint's voice never wavered—"why don't we stop pussyfooting around?"

Korsakov appeared to give it some thought, and then those wide shoulders shrugged under his long coat. "Simon," he said.

"So there we get to it then," Quint replied. It was such a relief to be discussing it in the open.

"Then that was indeed the formidable Charles Simon we've heard so much about," said Korsakov. He sounded annoyingly cheerful about it. "I can understand why he's eluded you for so long."

"Yeah, but I can't." Quint touched the eyepatch. "He was responsible for this, you know. Blew a building apart. Rained glass. Some got in my eye, sliced it to ribbons."

Korsakov shuddered, although whether it was in sympathy or just out of courtesy—or maybe even shaking with silent laughter—was something that Quint couldn't quite determine. "That must have been a hideous experience. I would not wish it on my worst enemy."

"Which means that I'm not your worst enemy?"

Korsakov laughed slightly. "You? You are my counterpart. To hate you would be to hate myself."

"Is hate required for someone to be an enemy?"

"For someone to be a truly superb enemy, yes. Simon, though, would make a truly superb tool."

"Oh, yes. Except he's displaying an amazing reluctance to be put into our toolbox," said Quint. "Our information is that you had some dealings with him in San Francisco."

"Your information would be correct," said Korsakov after a moment. "So the question becomes, how do we proceed?"

"It strikes me," said Quint slowly, "that this presents an intriguing hypothetical."

"Indeed?"

"Yes, the hypothetical being this: Wouldn't it be most interesting if the heads of two organizations such as ours—in order to apprehend an individual who has become extremely troublesome to both—were to work together?"

Korsakov raised an eyebrow. "Such talk of hypotheticals could be extremely dangerous. If you'd like, though . . . I could remove the danger, at least temporarily."

"Oh, really? Well . . . by all means."

Korsakov nodded slightly, and suddenly an extremely small gun had appeared in the palm of his hand, sliding out of his coat sleeve. Reflexively, and surprised, Quint started to reach for his own gun, but Korsakov didn't seem to be aware that he was there. Instead he angled the gun just slightly up and to his right, at hip level, and fired.

There was a gasp from nearby. Quint's head snapped around, just in time to see a man in the corner slumping to the ground. His hat fell over, exposing a mop of red hair.

"That's Fred Lassiter," said Quint in amazement.

"It *was* Fred Lassiter," was Korsakov's quiet correction.

"He's one of my people." His single eye widened in astonishment. "Genady, are you out of your mind?"

"In a sense. I was into his." He smiled mirthlessly. "It would seem that he was in Mr. Terwilliger's employ, unbeknownst to you. Shame on you, Quint. You're getting sloppy in your old age." Upon Quint's amazed look, he added, "Don't worry. The autopsy will read 'heart failure.' The bullet needle that contained the drug that killed him will dissolve in his bloodstream within thirty seconds. It, and the drug, will be utterly untraceable. That's just Mr. Terwilliger's bad luck, wouldn't you say? Oh . . . if I were you, I might make certain that Mr. Lassiter's computer medical profile makes mention of his history of heart problems. Just a suggestion."

"A good one," said Quint tonelessly. His mind was racing. He knew what the file said of Korsakov's mental powers. He might very well have been able to detect any such thoughts of complicity from Lassiter. Still, it might be a lie altogether, and Korsakov had just killed one of

Quint's men right in front of him, with total impunity. But . . . what motivation did Korsakov have to lie about all this?

"No motivation at all," said Korsakov, in response to Quint's unspoken thought. Quint fired him a look as, behind them, there were cries of alarm from passersby as they discovered the unmoving body of Lassiter.

Korsakov, for his part, seemed to have put the entire matter of Lassiter completely behind him. Instead he was pondering Quint's suggestion of teaming up. "Hmmm. Together. Now there is an intriguing idea. And what possible advantage could there be to such an unprecedented endeavor."

"I'd think it's obvious," replied Quint, making a herculean effort to steady his voice. "Simon's continued freedom has been an embarrassment to us. And now he's thrown one of his psychic monkey wrenches into your business as well. If we were to pool our resources, however . . . who knows what possibilities would be open to us?"

Genady Korsakov appraised Quint for a long moment. Then he took a step back, as if he were studying a portrait. "You are indeed serious, aren't you?"

"Never more so."

"And if we succeed . . . if Simon is apprehended . . . what do you propose we do then? Who gets him? Do we divide him like Solomon the Wise would?"

"Although it may sound like I'm putting you off, the bottom line is that I'm not certain what happens when it comes to that point. Cutting him in half might be the ideal solution, because that way he won't be around to bother either of us. He's become much too uncontrollable to be relied upon."

"Not too uncontrollable if you are contemplating surgery as an option," said Korsakov slowly. "I've heard that you have made tremendous advancements in lobotomy."

"We have," replied Quint. "How about this. We deal with who gets Simon when we come to that bridge—but we make a pact with each other that whoever does get Simon, we will never use him against our respective countries."

Korsakov laughed outright at that. "My dear Quint!" he boomed. "If I weren't able to discern for myself that you were serious, I'd think you're joking."

"Not at all. That would be one of our major concerns, after all. Besides, we each have plenty of enemies aside from each other."

"So tell me," said Korsakov. "If we were to acquire him, and we wanted to use him against your president, or your Mr. Terwilliger—this would not be permissible under the terms of your suggestion. Correct?"

Quint's single eye narrowed and hardened. "Everything's open for negotiation, Genady. Everything."

7

As night settled comfortably over the Coney Island shore, Googie made her way under the boardwalk with the dog called Zorro padding behind her. The only noise was the sand shifting beneath the great German shepherd's paws, and the soft *huff-huff* of his breath. The satchels on either side of his body were stuffed with the treasures that Googie had gotten from the supermarket, as were her own bags.

Hidden deep in the shadowed recesses under one pier was a large iron door, apparently rusted shut. Googie reached into her pocket and produced a key, which she inserted into the keyhole. As always, it was a slight strain for her to turn it, but she put her muscles into it and with the heavy sound of tumblers falling into place, the door unlatched. She swung it open and entered, Zorro right behind her.

The long hallway in front of her was illuminated with low wattage lamps strung along the way, and she swung the door shut behind her once she saw that Zorro was inside. She made her way down the hall, aware of the eyes upon her, secreted away in their hidden watch-points. Although she heard nothing, she was fully aware that her presence was being radioed ahead so that she wouldn't be challenged further on by someone caught off-guard.

She rounded a corner and stopped. Next to her, Zorro growled softly.

It was hard to call the man crouched in front of her a man. She wasn't sure how tall he was, because he was always squatting, like a toad on a lily pad. And this resemblance in posture was not the only one. His skin was brown, mottled, and extremely bumpy, and his eyes protruded slightly from their sockets. He had no eye-brows, or indeed bodily hair of any kind. His fingers and toes were elongated, and webbing had grown between them to give them a finned appearance. He tended to lick his lips in quick, sharp motions that made it seem as if he were checking the air for passing insects. Al-though she had never seen him eat a fly, she had little doubt that he was perfectly capable of it. His lips were thick and as tough-looking as the rest of his skin.

When he spoke, it was with a voice that was deep and gravelly, and seemed perpetually in a state of hiccuping. "You got something, Googie?" he asked, but the way he spoke, it came out sounding like "Yoouuu gOOOOTT sooomething, GOOOOgie?"

"Yeah, Horny," she told him. "I went shopping."

"You're our best forager," he told her. He moved closer, and there was something in his eyes that she def-initely didn't like, although she was used to it by now. Indeed, he looked at every female in Haven that way, so they were all used to it. When he'd first come to Haven, he'd called himself Toad for obvious reasons.

But as time had passed, he'd earned the sobriquet "Horny Toad."

It was understandable. It was hard to tell with someone like him, but as far as they could ascertain, he was about eighteen or nineteen. In a normal teenage boy, hormones were running rampant anyway. But at least the normal teenager has a shot at getting some action. Nobody in their right mind was so desperate to get laid that they'd invite Horny Toad into their bed, even though the sex lives of everyone who lived in Haven were their own business. So poor Horny Toad was stuck in a mode of perpetual frustration, and there seemed little chance of relief coming along anytime soon. In a way, Googie felt bad for him. Not bad enough to *do* anything about it, but she at least sympathized. It was more than those who simply couldn't stand the sight of him offered.

"Thanks, Horny," she said graciously. She walked past him and he started to follow right on her heels, the better for him to watch her backside and enjoy the play of her firm, hard ass beneath her cutoffs. But a warning growl from Zorro prompted him to drop back a few feet to a respectful distance.

Horny Toad glared at Zorro and contemplated taking some sort of action against him. As he thought of it, his mouth puckered and his cheeks moved, generating a wad of spit. But then he decided that something like that would probably anger Googie, and besides, unless he did something fatal to the animal, the creature would probably rip him in half in retaliation. It was preferable, he decided, to opt for the better part of valor; at least for the time being. Still, he did have the wad of spit in his mouth. He turned and spat it into a nearby corner, where it sizzled and sputtered, leaving a small, blackened hole where it had landed.

Googie made her way to the kitchen, and saw that Figurine was busy preparing dinner. Figurine turned when she heard them enter and smiled broadly.

It was hard not to like Figurine. She was open and honest, and the fact that she wore no clothes indicated that she was someone who had very little to hide.

The thing was, she was also translucent. The first time her psionic power had manifested itself, she had started to turn invisible. She had gotten halfway to that state and then panicked and stopped, afraid that she wouldn't be able to restore herself to visibility. She had been partly correct in that—she was now stuck in a semivisible state.

She was someone whom you might think you saw out of the corner of your eye, but if you weren't looking for her in a good light, or weren't looking at her from the correct angle, she would be nearly impossible to spot. Something of a free spirit even before she'd gotten stuck this way, she had shucked her clothes as soon as she'd gotten to Haven. Several of the more conservative members of the group had asked her to put some clothes on, but they had promptly been shouted down by other members of the Forsaken. And indeed, Figurine had such an outgoing air about her that even the ultraconservatives had eventually become relaxed about her casual nudity. When you saw it every day, the sensationalistic aspects of it tended to disappear.

No one was sure whether her perpetually "now you see me, now you don't" stage was physiological or psychological in its basis. Nor did it seem to matter; Figurine was perfectly happy in the state that she was in, so no one saw any need to analyze it to death.

When she spoke, it was with a honey-dripped southern accent. Since no one knew where she came from, it was difficult to decide whether she was putting it on or not—especially since it slipped occasionally if she was excited about something.

"Well now, how are y'all doing?" she said to the three individuals who had entered the kitchen. She walked over to them and crouched down in front of Zorro, scratching the top of his head. "And how's my puppy-wuppy today?"

"Your puppy-wuppy killed a couple of Pezzheads," Googie informed her.

Figurine gave a shrug of her shapely shoulders. "I'm sure he wouldn't have 'less he had to. Would you, puppy?" She nuzzled against him and Googie felt a faint taste of nausea coming on. Horny Toad just looked on enviously. If there was one female in the place he coveted more than any other, it was Figurine. Unfortunately for him, she was no more interested in satisfying him than anyone else in the place was. But at least she was considerably more polite about it.

Googie unloaded the burdened dog and, with Toad's help, dragged the full satchels over to the large larder table. She dumped the canned and packaged goods out and Figurine came over to inspect them. She nodded curtly and approvingly. "You're the best, honey. Absolutely the tiptop best."

"Thanks," said Googie flatly. She didn't particularly care what Figurine's opinion of her was, but a compliment was a compliment.

"Oh. The Magistrate wants to see you."

That surprised Googie. The Magistrate hadn't said

more than a half-dozen words to her in the past couple of months. It wasn't that he was upset with her or anything. He just tended not to waste words. He never chatted about anything, never kicked back and shot the breeze. When he did speak, it was in slow, measured tones, and usually in response to some immediate problem. Perhaps because he was the most powerful psionic she had ever met, and maybe the most powerful in the world, he felt a bit detached from the rest of them.

She felt a flash of guilty nervousness, although she didn't have the faintest idea why. She hadn't *done* anything to be nervous about. Still . . .

"Uh . . . okay, thanks, Fig," she said. She left the kitchen, leaving Horny Toad to ogle the apparently oblivious Figurine, and returned to her quarters quickly to freshen up. She washed the sweat of the day off briskly and, in a rare departure for her, splashed just a dash of perfume on herself. She didn't know why, but she did it. She turned to Zorro, said "Stay" firmly, and left him there.

She walked quickly to the Magistrate's chambers, nodding and greeting other members of the Forsaken as she went past. "Hey, Four-Eyes," she called at one point to a gangling young man. He nodded to her in acknowledgment, and the eye that was situated in his right temple winked at her. The one on the left temple was rolling about, not focused on anything in particular, and the two eyes that he possessed in the same place as most others were looking straight ahead.

She got to the Magistrate's chambers, knocked once, and waited for permission to enter.

"Come," came the notoriously crisp voice.

She entered, and saw him seated behind his desk,

skimming a thick bound volume; *Moby Dick*, it appeared to be. He said nothing to her at first, apparently caught up in what he was reading. It gave her a few moments to compose herself and flush away her nervousness. Perhaps that had been his intention.

His hair was dead white and cropped very short, almost a crew cut. His eyebrows were white as well. His face was narrow and hard, and a white, neatly trimmed beard lined his jaw. His eyes were dark green. His neck, like the rest of his body, was slender. He was dressed in dark shades of purple, his preferred color. She had never understood why, but as far back as she could remember, it was what he had worn.

"Expedition went well?" he asked before he looked up from his book. Then he closed it with a firm *thwap* and looked up at her. His gaze seemed to cut right through her.

"Fine. Just fine."

"Zorro a help?"

"Oh, yeah. He's been great, ever since I got him."

"I see." He steepled his fingers and then said, "If I said to get rid of him, would you?"

She didn't hesitate. "Yes, sir."

"I see."

"But I would leave with him."

"I see," he said again, in exactly the same tone. He paused a moment, considering the situation. "Oracle spoke with me."

"Did she?" Googie frowned at that. Everyone in Haven knew Oracle. They referred to her as old blood and guts, for her tendency to slice open the entrails of animals in order to do her readings of the future. In the old days, of course, women such as her had utilized sheep or such. Nowadays, she had to depend upon rats that she caught in her mercy traps. She claimed that she could get just as accurate readings with the rats. A number of the Forsaken were of the opinion that she didn't need any animals at all—that she just did all that for show.

What nobody disputed was the accuracy of her castings, which meant that if Oracle had said something, then attention had to be paid. "What did"—and she cleared her throat—"what did Oracle say?"

"She said that the dog was a major focal point. She said that the dog's owner was going to come searching for it."

"Impossible," she said flatly. "Brainpan wiped him. There's no way he's going to remember anything."

"Never say never," he replied. He didn't speak in a rush, but in careful, measured tones. "What one person does, another can undo. Oracle says the dog's owner will show up. And there will be major difficulties when he does."

"So"—she licked her lips nervously—"so what are you saying? That I should get rid of him to avoid trouble?"

"That will not help," he said. "The future is set. The owner will come. It cannot be avoided. What will happen beyond that, Oracle could not discern. You must be prepared for the possibility of relinquishing the dog."

"Are you going to force me to?"

"I have not decided. I shall weigh the evidence when the time comes. That's all."

"But what if—?"

"That's all," he repeated, more firmly this time. Then, as if she had already left, he returned to his book.

Her jaw moved speechlessly and then, realizing that

further discussion would be pointless, she turned and started to walk out when a voice said, "Googie."

She stopped and looked back at him. She couldn't recall him ever addressing her by name. It sounded oddly personal, coming from him. "Yeah?"

"We take care of our own here." Then he once again returned to his book, and it was clear that the discussion was over.

She bobbed her head gratefully, and then returned to her room. When she got there, Brainpan was waiting for her.

Brainpan was a good ten years older than Googie, and had already lost most of his hair. This left him with a very pronounced forehead, and his eyes seemed to glitter from beneath his distended brows. When he moved, it was with meticulous and unwasteful gestures, an absolute economy of motion.

He was holding Zorro's muzzle in his hands and staring into the animal's eyes. There were only three people in the world that Zorro let touch him—one was Googie, the second was Fig, and the third was Brainpan.

"What're you doing?" asked Googie.

He didn't even look up at her. "There was some sort of interruption to his thought process," he said. "For a brief moment, he connected with his origins."

"What're you saying? That he was remembering?"

Brainpan rose to face her. "Not just him," he said. "For a few seconds there, his previous owner must have started to remember who he was. The moment he did, the link he has with the dog started to kick in."

She looked helplessly from Zorro back to Brainpan. "Well . . . well what are we going to do?"

"I just gave him a booster," said Brainpan. "I'd do

the same to the previous owner if he were here, but he's not. And as long as he's not, there's nothing I can do."

She sagged down onto a couch and looked at Zorro dismally. "The Magistrate says his previous owner is going to come after him."

"That's a possibility," admitted Brainpan.

"Well, if he does . . . what're we going to do? Can you wipe him again?"

"Yes, but if he's got a strong mind, his memory could come back yet again. It won't solve the problem. Unless . . ."

His voice trailed off, and she did not miss her cue. "Unless what?"

Brainpan looked down, as if interested in his spotlessly shined shoes, and when he looked up it was with an almost-mischievous grin on his face. "I'd have to turn him into a vegetable. He'd be alive, but he'd spend the rest of his life in a complete fog. Irreparable. Brain cells would actually be destroyed. I don't like to do it. It makes me feel very uncomfortable, and it's something of a strain. But I can if I have to."

She went to him and took his hand. "Please," she said softly, urgently. "I love Zorro. He's my best friend. It would kill me to have to return him, or have him taken away."

"Well . . . it's possible, as I said. If I had the proper . . . incentive, of course."

She knew exactly what he was talking about.

She turned to the dog and said, "Zorro. Go out. Wait outside for a while."

Zorro stood there, staring at her. She got up, went to him, and escorted him to the door, closing it behind him. When she turned, Brainpan had already pulled off his shirt. Googie sighed inwardly and gave a mental shrug. Brainpan had a lean, muscular body, even if he did have a creepy gaze. She could do worse.

She went to him and insinuated her body against his. Because barter was the way of the Forsaken.

8

The sun's morning rays streamed through the prism that dangled in front of Chuck Simon's eyes.

The colors danced across his face and seemed to transform the entire world into a shimmering array of rainbow patterns. And through those patterns danced all sorts of faces and images, none of which he could place. Images that seemed so close and yet, frustratingly, so far off. He saw a building that looked like a school, with teens emerging and waving, and he fought the impulse to wave back. He saw tall buildings with glass exploding from them, and then there was a circus, and he could almost smell the sawdust and the air heavy with animal scents. And there was a woman balanced on a tightrope, and then another woman dressed in khaki, and a towering forest, and . . .

A duck?

Some sort of huge duck, and then the face of a tortured and angry young boy, and a bridge, and then the cold of water surrounding him . . .

And a train, a train moving at incredible speeds, and

some sort of monster with false faces, and a woman . . .

A beautiful woman. More than any of the others he had seen, this one made his heart ache.

All experiences that seemed as if they had happened to someone else. Yet he knew that they were his own. He had been told so by Alex; that he would see things that he himself had witnessed. And still he had trouble believing them or understanding them, because he seemed so removed from them.

"Chuck," came Alex's voice, soft and modulated. "Chuck, do you hear me? Do you hear me, Chuck?"

"Yes," he said.

The prism twirled in her hands. It had been ages since Alex had done anything like this—not since her days as a psych student in the university. But when she had done it, she had excelled, and there was no reason on earth that she couldn't do it again. "Chuck . . . I want you to remember."

"Remember."

"Yes, remember, Chuck. Remember what happened to you. Remember where you came from."

"Remember."

"What is your name?"

"Chuck Simon."

"Where were you born?"

"I don't remember."

"How do you know your name is Chuck Simon?"

"You told me so."

She sighed. This was beyond a simple mental block. Whoever had done this to Chuck had been extremely thorough. If she ever met him, she wasn't sure whether she'd congratulate him on a job well done or just kill him.

She decided that rather than try to dredge up all his long-term memories, she would concentrate on the short term. On what had happened to cause him to be like this. And she thought she knew how to do it: by calling on the closest link and relationship that Chuck seemed to have in this world.

"Chuck . . . I want you to picture Rommel."

"Rommel?"

"Your dog. The big one. The very big one, with the 'Z' shape in his fur. The one you talk to."

The light glittered in his eyes, and seemed to reshape itself into the outline of a muzzle. And there were two ears, sticking up, and dark eyes that had both menace and devotion in them. And dark fur with a "Z" in it . . .

"Rommel," he said softly. He felt as if he could reach out and touch the memory.

"Rommel," she affirmed. "When was the last time you saw Rommel?"

"They took Rommel." The outrage and the hurt seemed to bubble from nowhere. "They took Rommel. They made him leave. He wouldn't have left me if they hadn't made him."

He sounded like an angry child, deprived of his best friend in the world. Perhaps, to a degree, that's what he was.

"Who took him?" asked Alex.

"They did."

"Who?"

"The ones I wanted to find." He wasn't even fully aware of what he was saying. The memories were coming from beyond his conscious recollection, exactly as Alex hoped would happen.

"Who did you want to find?"

"Haven."

"Haven?" said Alex in confusion. "Who is Haven? Who is Haven, Chuck?"

"Not who. Where. It's a place. A safe place. I heard about it . . . but it's not safe. Not if they took Rommel away."

"A safe place for whom?"

"Psionics."

For a moment her mind reeled at the concept. A safe place? A whole nest of them? Maybe even some sort of community? My God! The collective power that such a grouping would represent. Who knew what they were capable of, or what they could accomplish if they were handled by the right people. People like . . .

Like herself? And what was she supposed to do if she did find them? Recruit them to her organization? Except her organization wanted her dead.

Besides, she wasn't quite so sure at this point that she would *want* her side—or what was nominally her side— to have that much power at their disposal. If there was one thing she was learning pretty damned quickly, it was that the balance of power was even more precarious than she would have thought.

Whatever she decided, first things had to be first.

"Chuck," she said softly. "Where is Haven?"

And that was when the back window crashed in.

Alex spun as the female bikers came pouring in, their feet crunching the shattered glass. The daylight back-lighted them, making them look like an army of dark angels as they stormed in, whooping and hollering.

"I knew it!" shouted the one who had been in the lead—the one who had gotten herself knocked around by the RAC 3000. "I knew there had to be someone in here, with Supercar parked outside! Get her! Get the meat!"

Alex cast a desperate glance at the bag in which she had her weaponry packed. She took a breath and lunged for it, but the bikers were already there, in between Alex and her goal.

"Coney Island," Chuck was quietly muttering. "Coney Island. In Coney Island." He was staring straight ahead, oblivious of what was happening. Even though Alex had dropped the prism, he was still caught up in his hypnotic haze.

"This one wants to go to the beach!" shouted the leader, and ignored him momentarily to turn her gaze on Alex. Alex, for her part, was struggling in the grasp of three of the large women, two of whom had her arms pinned and the third with her arms wrapped around Alex's legs. Alex fought fiercely, but she had been unable to get any leverage.

The leader approached her slowly, grinning. Alex's gaze was drawn to a fierce scar across her forehead. Someone had come close to spilling her brains all over the landscape. Just Alex's luck that the attempt had been unsuccessful.

"I'm Mu," said the leader, pronouncing it "Mew."

Alex frowned in confusion. "You're me?"

She grinned a toothy grin. "I get that all the time. I . . . am . . . Mu. And you—?"

"I am me," replied Alex, casting a desperate glance at Chuck. He seemed off in his own little world, which in fact he pretty much was. "Look, I don't mean to be hidebound or anything, but this is, y'know, private property. So maybe it would be better for everyone involved if you, like, got the hell out?"

"Oh, I'll tell you what would be better, meat," said Mu. She reached out and cupped Alex's chin in one hand. Alex forced herself not to look away, but instead glowered at her fiercely. "In fact . . . I'll show you what's better. You and your little space cadet friend." She cast a disdainful glance at Chuck, who kept muttering to himself. "What's his problem? Coney Island? What the hell is he talking about?"

"Chuck!" shouted Alex, feeling that her time to make any sort of move was rapidly vanishing. "Chuck, please! Do something!"

"Him?" Mu laughed, and the others joined in. "He doesn't look to me like he's got any real plans lined up against us."

Mu sauntered over to Chuck and grabbed him by the shoulder, hauling him to his feet. He blinked in confusion, his mind in a haze. "Alex—?" he murmured.

"No, it's not Alex," grinned Mu toothily, and she reached down with her free hand and grabbed Chuck by the crotch. Her steely fingers closed firmly.

From across the room, Alex grimaced and turned away as Chuck let out a screech.

And then he let out a hell of a lot more, as a wave of psionic energy rolled from him, hoisting Mu completely off her feet and sending her spiraling upward. She smashed into the ceiling and richocheted off it like a pinball, crashing to the ground. She lay there unmoving, blood rapidly matting her hair.

Chuck staggered, bent over double, pain stabbing through every part of his body. Distantly he heard the shouts of *"Get him!"* and he didn't know what to do, or how to function. The hand-to-hand combat that had come so naturally and unexpectedly to him wasn't entirely possible right now, because it was agony to even *think* about standing up, much less doing it. But his mind . . . his mind was working just fine.

He didn't know how to consciously trigger the power that he wanted to use. It simply happened. He lashed out toward the sounds of pounding feet, not deliberately trying to use his TK power, but instead simply thinking *Keep away! Stay away!* Thought, in his case, was literally deed, as the women were thrown back in all directions, buffeted by something that they couldn't see, couldn't hear, but by God they could feel it. It was as if a giant hand had swung out and, like swatting a fly, had smacked them all away.

Two were blown back out of the window they had come in. The rest of them were tossed against walls or the ceiling, and one just skidded across the carpet like a hockey puck.

The women holding Alex looked on in shock. Alex made her move. She elbowed one aside, turned, grabbed the other by the neck, and flipped her across her body. The one who had been holding her legs, Alex promptly kneed right in the face.

Abruptly there was a roar of a high-powered engine, coming closer by the second, and then the front door of the house blew in with a splintering of wood and metal. In the doorway, honking and revving, was the front of the RAC 3000. The threshold wasn't wide enough for the car to get through, but then the RAC 3000 backed up and proceeded to make another charge in a single-minded endeavor to smash her way into the house.

The Cycle Sluts didn't hang out to learn whether the car was successful or not. Grabbing up the fallen Mu, and the two other members that had been knocked cold by the impact, the Cycle Sluts beat a hasty retreat out the back. Alex heard the powerful motorcycle engines rev up, and realized that they must have shut the cycles down and walked them the last block or two in order to sneak up on the inhabitants of the house. Now, though, they were not wasting any time in getting the hell out of there.

Alex went to Chuck, who was still lying on the ground, curled in a fetal position and groaning. For a brief moment she was afraid to get near him, for fear that he would thoughtlessly reach out and knock her around too, the way he had the cyclists. But she put it aside, demanding of herself that she have more nerve than that. "Chuck," she said urgently. "Chuck, are you all right?"

Through a haze of pain he looked up at her. "Is this . . . part of the therapy?" he managed to get out.

She tried not to laugh, because he didn't seem in the position to appreciate whatever humor she might find in the situation. "I'm so sorry, Chuck. Do you remember anything?"

"There were . . ." He squinted, and tears rolled down the sides of his face. "There were some women here. One of them hurt me. It's weird. Usually I do so well with women."

"Just some bad chemistry," Alex told him. "They didn't feel like being charmed."

"They didn't have to worry."

"Can you stand?"

"Not without screaming."

"Then stay like that until you can."

"Deal."

It was five long minutes before Chuck felt strong or

steady enough to stand up, and even then he was leaning on Alex's shoulder. "I think those women had an attitude problem," he said.

"Considering that just the other day it was a bunch of men who were trying to kill me in an alleyway, I'd say the whole world has an attitude problem. Come on. Walk it off. One and two and . . ." She proceeded to lead him around the room until he felt the strength returning to his legs, and the pain was fading to a distant ache.

She patted him on the chest and helped him to sit. "I think we'd better get out of here soon, before more friends come back. Do you remember anything of what you said or saw?"

He rubbed his temples. "Just a lot of images. Familiar faces. But nothing I can latch on to."

"That's okay. You said two things I could latch on to. One was 'Haven.' The other was 'Coney Island.' "

He thought about it a moment. "Yeah," he said slowly. "Yeah, that . . . that sounds familiar. That sounds real familiar. I don't know where, or how. I remember . . . some guys. And they . . ." His voice trailed off, and then he shook his head. "It's gone. Whatever it was, it's gone."

"Maybe it's gone," said Alex firmly, "but we know where it went. Come on."

"Where are we going?"

"Where else?" she said, packing up the bag. The RAC 3000 had already withdrawn from the front door, although the door was bashed up enough that it wasn't going to be in working order again anytime soon. "Coney Island. To find Haven."

9

Sometime Earlier . . .

Dr. Martin Faber walked up to the bed of his latest patient and leaned over, smiling sympathetically. "How are we doing today, Reuel?" he asked.

Beutel smiled coldly. "Fine, Doctor. Yourself?"

Faber beamed at him. "Why, just fine, Reuel. Thank you for asking. So . . . do you think you're going to be able to sit up today?"

"I think so."

"Good. Good." Faber marked something on his ever-present clipboard. "I must tell you, Reuel, I'm thrilled with your progress."

"Doctor . . . I'd like to see a mirror, if you don't mind."

"A mirror?" Faber frowned slightly at that. "Now that's a curious request, Reuel."

"Not so curious." His voice, still gravelly, at least bore some resemblance to his own. "I know a lot of work was done on me. I'm entitled to see. Also . . . I'd like to be unstrapped."

Faber shook his head firmly. "Now we definitely can't

allow that, Reuel. I've been over this with you before."

"Doctor," and he tried to sound as reasonable—even sympathetic—as he could. "Doctor, I know you're trying not to upset me. But has it occurred to you that by keeping me trussed up . . . by refusing to let me do something as simple as look at my reflection . . . you're not doing anything that will help me recover? You're making me afraid of the truth," and he added a convincing tremor in his voice.

"I just wanted to make certain you are ready, Reuel. That's all."

"I'm ready," said Beutel. He was tired of looking face up. He was tired of his body covered by a blanket, and not having any sensation from the neck down . . . or from the neck up, for that matter. It was like lying inside a corpse.

Faber sighed once. "All right. This is against my better judgment, but if you're sure . . ."

"Oh, I'm sure."

Faber nodded, and then went out of the room for a moment. When he returned, he was holding a mirror in one hand. He held it up in front of Beutel's face.

A head swathed in white bandages looked back at him. Only his eyes and mouth were visible. "Take the bandages off, Doc," said Beutel.

"I don't think that—"

"Goddammit, Doc!" said Beutel, momentarily losing control. He closed his eyes for a moment to compose himself and when he spoke again, it was with extraordinary calm. "Doc, you have no idea of the shit I've been through. You have no idea of the things I've seen. No matter what's been done to it, I can stand to see my face. Okay?"

Faber pursed his lips for a moment, and then disappeared again. When he returned, he was holding sheers. Without a word he set to work snipping away at the bandages. He had placed the mirror facedown so that he had both hands free to do the cutting, and within moments he had removed the gauze obstructions from Beutel's face. He stepped back, nodded approvingly for a moment, then reached down for the mirror.

Before he held it up, though, he said slowly, "Remember, Reuel . . . it's somewhat drastic."

He raised the mirror up in front of Beutel's face.

Beutel hadn't been entirely certain what to expect, but it sure wasn't this. "What is this, a joke?" he asked. "You've got me in metal bandages?"

"No, Reuel," said Faber softly.

Beutel stared again. Stared for a good long time.

There were his eyes, all right, and the bridge of his nose between them. There was his mouth. Both of them were neatly boxed by metal.

In terms of the rest of his face, it took very little time to check out. There was no rest of his face.

The rest of him was gleaming metal.

"Doc," he said slowly, "get this goddamned coffee maker off my head." He saw his mouth moving when he spoke, but it was like watching something or someone else. Something not remotely human.

"Reuel," he said, "you have to understand . . . your face, your head was . . ."

He had no ears. Instead there were several little holes on either side of his head that looked like built-in microphones. There was no nose—that was smoothed over completely. Just that little nub of his nose between his eyes, and that was all.

"What about the rest of me?" said Beutel slowly.

"There was similar damage. It's a miracle that you're even . . ."

"It's fine, Doc," said Beutel. "Really. Now, y'see . . . a lesser person might think that you did all this to me because you wanted to see if you could. That you took this opportunity to make me into your own personal guinea pig."

He spoke with such chilling calm that Faber realized he would have preferred it if Beutel had been screaming at him. "Reuel . . . I know this is a shock . . ."

"No . . . honest, Doc," said Beutel, and he actually sounded mirthful. "This is . . . this has real possibilities. Look . . ." and he raised his head. It had been the first actual display of motion he'd exhibited since coming to. "Just seeing the work, the craftsmanship you've put into this . . . like I said, a lesser person would think that, but not me. Oh, no, Doc. Not me. Lemme see the rest. Honest to God," and he could barely keep the excitement out of his voice. He sounded like a child on Christmas morning.

At first Faber wasn't sure to trust it. Beutel was adjusting incredibly quickly. For that matter, he might not even be adjusting. He might be denying it, refusing to accept the evidence of his own eyes.

But on the other hand . . . Beutel was a trained agent of the Complex. As he had said himself, he was accustomed to dealing with extraordinary circumstances, even when those circumstances involved himself.

"All right, Reuel," he said. He reached down and pulled back the sheet that was covering Beutel's body.

He stared down at what appeared to be a living machine. A robot, out of some old science fiction movie.

Everywhere, everywhere he looked was gleaming metal. He looked down at his hands, his feet. Everything was that organic metal that had once constituted only his right hand. Heavy metal bonds were at his arms and legs, and one across his chest. Strapped tautly across him, they were what had kept him immobile.

He flexed the fingers of his new hands, moved the feet that swiveled on the ankle extensions. The only seams visible were those that constituted joints. Everywhere else was smooth. Even his crotch.

Beutel's mouth smiled.

"Not much of me left, was there?" he said very, very softly.

"As I already said," said Faber, slowly lowering the blanket. "Internal organs, skeletal structure . . . we did the best we could, Reuel. All of your bodily functions are now self-contained. You're very different from what you were. On the other hand, your potential is immeasurable."

Beutel looked up at him hopefully. "You really think so?"

"Absolutely." And Faber gave a big smile.

That was when Beutel reached out with his mind, and the scissors that Faber had used to slice open the bandages floated up from the bed. Then they spun in the air, shot forward, and buried themselves squarely in Faber's throat.

Faber tried to shriek, but his vocal cords had been cut. Instead he gurgled up his own blood, his eyes bulging out and strangled *urkh-urkh* sounds emerging from his mouth. His hands flailed about, his first instinct to yank out the scissors but his medical training telling him that that was the absolute wrong move. He made it anyway, grabbed for the scissors and yanked them out. Blood poured from his throat and down the front of his shirt, hot and welcome to Beutel, who chuckled softly to himself as he once again seized hold of the scissors with his mind, yanked them from Faber's spasmodic grasp, and plunged them straight into the middle of Faber's head.

The impact sent him stumbling back and he hit the floor, knocking over a water pitcher on a nearby dresser. The ice water spilled out onto the floor, turning deep red.

Beutel took distracted note of Faber's death gurgle as he focused his full concentration on the bonds that were restraining him. He put the power of his mind to them, along with the strength in his cybernetic body. He supposed that he could have done it earlier, but he simply wasn't ready. Now, though, he most definitely was.

There was a protesting squeal of metal and then the bonds gave way. Beutel sat up so quickly that he almost hurled himself out of the bed when he did so. He took a moment to compose himself and noticed—because he was always so attuned to himself—that there was no excitement in him. Usually when he was committing some act of violence—murder, mayhem, etc.—his pulse sped up, his breathing became rapid. He became excited, aroused . . .

Ah, but his arousal equipment had gone south, hadn't it. Didn't have to worry about that anymore. Everything was self-contained now, just like the old doc had mentioned.

Now there was no quickening, there was no rush. There was simple, icy precision. Unhurried. Unmussed, unfussed. Indeed, that might be an improvement. After all, it had been his haste and his allowing Simon to get under his skin that had led to his previous defeats. That wasn't going to happen this time, though.

"Thanks, Doc," he said to the body on the floor.

He started to move, and his movements seemed slow and clumsy. Ponderous. He felt like a walking tank. He wasn't going to be taking mambo lessons anytime soon, but on the other hand, it was probably going to be worth it.

Also, his every step began to feel more and more smooth. It was as if something inside him—automatic gyros or some sort of Faber-installed balancing system— was enabling him to become more comfortable with every passing moment. It was like going from crawling to walking in a matter of seconds.

He moved noiselessly. He thought he would hear some sort of servos or machinelike humming, but there was nothing, except the faint clacking of his metal-padded feet on the shining floor.

He stepped out into the hallway and immediately caught the attention of the nurse whose face had been the first thing he'd seen. She was standing nearby a nurse's station, talking with a man in a dark suit, whom Beutel immediately recognized as agent Tillis from the Complex.

Tillis's eyes widened and he immediately started toward Beutel, pulling his gun from his shoulder holster. The nurse was picking up a phone as Tillis said slowly, "All right, Reuel . . . take it easy and get back into bed."

Beutel stepped forward quickly, not even bothering to use his TK power against Tillis. He wanted to see just what his body could do.

The first thing it did was effortlessly deflect a direct

hit from the gun of the alarmed Tillis, who had not hesitated to fire when he saw the look in Beutel's eyes. The first bullet bounced off Beutel's chest, and the second off the upper arm that he was holding in front of his face, protecting the vulnerable eyes and mouth. The last thing he wanted to do was literally swallow a bullet.

Beutel swung a fist in leisurely fashion, and it moved so quickly that he misjudged the distance and completely missed Tillis, who stepped to the side and fired again into Beutel's middle. A small scuff mark was left on the metal, but that was all.

Beutel swung again, and this time he did not miss. He was extremely pleased with the result—the powered fist caved in Tillis's forehead. Tillis hit the ground and Beutel, out of curiosity, stepped on Tillis's chest. His foot went straight through to the floor, impressing Beutel with the weight of his new body. It didn't feel that heavy to move anymore, indicating that whatever systems were powering it were certainly doing the job. It had a fierce effect on whatever he encountered, though, evidenced by the fact that he stepped away from Tillis and left a trail of bloody footprints behind himself.

He spotted the nurse nearby the station, the phone having fallen to the floor. There was blood trickling down her face and she was ashen. Beutel realized that she must have caught a ricochet. She was fighting with everything she had to avoid sliding to the floor, clutching to the edge of the counter with all her strength.

"Help me," she whispered to Beutel.

He took her face in his hands and kissed her. "All right, darling," he said, and snapped her neck with a marvelously quick, efficient gesture. He allowed her to slide to the floor as he looked at his hands in pleasure. "Oh, yeah," he said. "I could definitely get used to this."

He walked back to Tillis, rummaged in his pockets until he found Tillis's car keys and registration, and headed out to the parking lot to go on about his business.

10

The RAC 3000 made its way slowly through the streets of Coney Island, sensors on full. Alex was in the driver's seat, and Chuck watched out the passenger window.

Alex was letting the RAC do the driving, so that she could have both her hands free if she needed to fire a weapon. The guns that she had taken off the various agents who had tried to kill her were piled in the seat next to her. They made a rather impressive little collection.

She glanced warily at Chuck. He had been extremely quiet since they had left Queens, and she had wanted desperately to know what was going through his mind. The hypnosis had breached the blockade that had been put into his mind. But the memories had not come flooding back. Instead they were trickling in, with a slow, steady drip.

He turned and looked at her, as if seeing her for the first time. "You were a reporter, weren't you?"

She smiled inwardly. In another life, she had been. In

a cover identity under which she had hidden herself. It had been that identity in which she first met Chuck Simon.

"Yeah," she said. She watched the street carefully in front of them, and said, "Rac . . . you smell anything?"

"I do not have any olfactory capabilities," the RAC 3000 informed her. The car sounded slightly piqued. Alex had come to notice that the car actually sounded a tad annoyed whenever it was reminded of capabilities it didn't possess.

"Sensors then?"

"I do not detect any disruptive or unusual aspects in the environment. However, if I do, Alexandra, I will inform you immediately. Interrogatives are not necessary."

"So you'll tell me when you're damned good and ready."

"That is correct."

"Hold it."

The command had come from Chuck, and it was the first time since she had encountered him that he sounded at all decisive, like his old self.

"Hold what, Charles?" inquired the car.

But Alex understood immediately. "Stop the car, Rac."

"I *am* the car."

"Then stop yourself."

The RAC 3000 obediently slowed to a halt. They were directly opposite a supermarket, and Chuck stared at it for a long moment. Then he pulled at the door release, but it wouldn't open.

Alex had given the RAC 3000 an instruction to keep Chuck's door locked, because she wasn't entirely sure what he might do at any given time. For all she knew, he might leap out if the mood struck him. Of course, if his psionic powers kicked in fully, and he regained control over them instead of just when he was prompted under some sort of reflex action, then she couldn't keep him in the car no matter what. "Let him out, Rac," said Alex.

The door obediently swung open and Chuck stepped out. He stood there for a moment next to the car, staring at the supermarket, his face a mask of concentration. It was as if he was trying to remember something that hadn't even been in his personal experience.

Slowly he waggled a finger as if scolding someone. "Something happened here," he said.

"Something? Something like what?"

"I don't know."

He started across the street, and when Alex called his name, he ignored her. Within moments he was inside the store, and he gagged on the stench that filled the air.

Forcing himself to ignore the smell, he started walking up one aisle and down the next. There was a faint buzzing in the back of his head. Nothing that he could easily put his finger on, but it was there all the same.

Then, at the end of one aisle, he saw a mass of redness. Instinctively he knew what it was: blood. Something extremely violent had happened here, but he wasn't sure exactly what.

Slowly he walked to the far end of the aisle. Something made him position his hands in a defensive posture that he didn't fully understand, but knew immediately was correct. By the time he got close to the blood smears, he wasn't even walking in normal fashion. Instead he was walking with one foot in the lead, pulling him forward in a stealthy, cautious manner. His weight was primarily on his back leg, allowing maximum maneuverability for the lead leg.

He studied the smears on the floor. Whatever had happened here had been cleaned up to some degree. There had been bodies, to be sure, but now they were gone. Tidied up. How nice, since company was coming.

"Okay," he said softly. "Okay. What happened here?"

Then he heard something, apparently from the next aisle over. Some sort of steady dripping sound.

He walked quickly around the aisle and stopped short. His lips drew back in disgust.

Situated on the shelf was a human head. He only caught a quick glimpse, because he looked away very quickly from the hideous sight. It looked to be a young man, and the skin around the bottom of the throat was jagged. The eyes were open and rolled upward, as if the head had been in the process of giving a final sigh of annoyance when torn from its shoulders. The dripping sound that Chuck had heard had been from the blood, naturally.

"Alex!" he shouted, and then he heard a screech. It was barely in time to alert him as someone leaped over the top of the shelves, slamming into him and knocking him to the ground.

But Chuck immediately twisted and managed to hurl the attacker off himself. And there was more than just providing a defense this time. Chuck was moving with quickness and confidence that he hadn't been feeling earlier. There was something about this place, a presence that he couldn't name, that was giving him a certainty in what he was doing. Certainly it was filled with gore and violence . . . but then again, that's what his life had become as of late.

He put out a hand and stopped the assailant in his tracks without touching him. It was a teenager, all right, his face bizarrely painted, his hair looking as if it had been cut with a weed whacker. He shrieked in frustration and trembled, waving his fists around and demanding to be released. For Chuck, it was a good feeling. He was deliberately applying this power that he had, and it felt good. Damned good. It was as if adrenaline were pouring through every vein.

"You can struggle all you want," said Chuck archly. "But you're not going anywhere unless I decide to let you go."

There was the sound of running feet, and for a moment, Chuck wondered if he was going to have to deal with others as well. But it turned out to be Alex, looking confused but determined. She had a gun in either hand, and was immediately checking the area for potential danger. She stared at the guy that Chuck was holding immobile, and nodded in quick approval. "Looks like you're getting the hang of it," she observed.

He didn't reply. Instead he focused on the young punk. "Who are you?" he demanded.

"Who . . . who are you?!" squeaked the prisoner. He was thoroughly spooked by the fact that he was being kept immobile by nothing that was visible.

"My name is Chuck," said Chuck. "Okay. Now who are you, and what happened here?"

"Huh . . . Hannibal. I'm . . . Hannibal." He looked like it was a strain to recall his name, and Alex was able to tell from the look in his eyes that his body was so filled with illegal substances that if he urinated in the Hudson River he could light up New Jersey.

"Hannibal," and Alex went to him and took him firmly by the ear. Mostly she wanted to see if any nerve endings were still functioning. She was rewarded with a terrified yelp. "Hannibal, you're going to tell us what went down here. There's blood everywhere. Why is there blood everywhere?"

"I don't know."

"Tell me about the dog," she said.

Chuck fired her a look of surprise. "What? How do you know there was a dog involved with any of this?"

She nodded in the direction of the puddles of blood. "Check it out. Paw prints. Big mother, too. Bet it's yours."

He turned to look, and sure enough, in some sections of the huge bloodstains there were paw prints. Some animal had gone running through the blood. Chances were that some animal had actually caused the blood, and judging from the size of the prints, it could very well be the same animal.

"There was no dog!" said the Pezzhead with certainty. "It was . . . it was a lion! I'm tellin' ya!"

"Where'd you see it?" demanded Chuck. Unconsciously, he squeezed tighter and the Pezzhead shrieked.

"It was with a girl, man! I mean it! I was standing guard outside, and she knocked me out with some sort of gun. I was just coming to when she came out, and I was gonna get up and go for her when I saw the . . . the thing she was with. I knew if I made any kind of move, it would come after me, man. So I stayed put. Absolutely put. It didn't see me, man. Didn't care about me. Didn't do nothing to me. I was quiet as an itty-bitty mouse."

"Oh, I'm sure you were," said Chuck.

"But it was a lion! I swear! Or maybe a bear! Or a moose!"

Alex nodded. "It's an understandable mistake, if he saw who . . . what . . . I think he saw. Did it have a thing in its fur?"

"Thing?" He looked at her uncomprehendingly.

"A 'Z' shape. In its fur, on its forehead." Alex traced the letter "Z" on her own forehead. Chuck looked at her in surprise.

"I don't know," said the Pezzhead in futility. "I don't know."

"The girl. Where'd she come from?"

"I don't know . . ."

"I'm getting tired of hearing that," said Alex, and she took one of the Pezzhead's hands firmly. She grasped his index finger and started to pull down on it, and he shrieked. Chuck looked at her worriedly, but she ignored him. "Now listen carefully. You will answer my questions, and for every answer I don't like, you lose the feeling in a finger. Get it?"

"Alex," said Chuck warningly.

Again she paid no attention. "The girl. Where did she come from?"

"I don't *know!*" he wailed.

She started to bend his finger back. Chuck stood there, confused and unsure.

"Take a guess," she said.

"All right! All right! Uh . . ." And he really did seem to be trying most desperately to come up with an answer. Any answer. "Uh . . . she, uh . . . she could be one of the Freaks."

"Freaks?" Alex looked at Chuck, who shrugged. "What freaks?"

"It's a gang. It's the weirdest gang, man. They live near the boardwalk somewhere, and they can all do things. Weird shit. I swear. I swear. She has to be one of those Freaks. I mean, who else would go around with a lion?"

"Who indeed?" asked Alex thoughtfully. "Chuck, you can let him go."

"Oh, can I really?" said Chuck, making no attempt to hide his sarcasm. Mentally he released the grip and the Pezzhead shrunk away from him, gibbering helplessly.

"You're going to take us there," said Alex, stabbing a finger at him.

"No! I don't know where they are! I swear!" And suddenly he dodged around Alex and bolted for the door.

Quickly she turned to Chuck. "Stop him!"

But Chuck merely stood there as the frantic Pezzhead dashed out the door, crying and sobbing hysterically. Not making any effort to hide her annoyance, Alex said, "Why the hell didn't you stop him?"

"Because we got everything out of him that we were going to," said Chuck. "He wasn't lying. He doesn't know where these so-called Freaks are."

"How do you know?"

"I just do. I can sense he was telling the truth."

"Oh, great." Alex's hands slapped against her sides. "Pick up things by thinking about them, read minds. Houdini Junior here."

"Pardon me for knowing when someone isn't lying. I doubt it would be much good in your profession."

"You're right. I always assume that everyone is lying. It saves time that way."

"Come on," he said, gesturing to her as he headed toward the door. "Let's get to the boardwalk. See if we can find these 'Freaks.'"

Before she could say anything else, he was out the door. Oh, his confidence was returning, all right. In leaps and bounds.

As much as she had wanted to help him, she found herself nostalgic for when she had been in charge.

11

The waters of the ocean crashed against the shore, and Chuck stood there and tried to imagine what it was like to have scores of bathers and young families, running and jumping and laughing as if they didn't have a care in the world.

He wondered how anyone could possibly not have a care in the world. To merely exist in the world was to be weighted down with more cares than anyone could possibly believe. To escape them for even a few moments seemed an impossibility.

Even though there were glimmerings of his past, flashes, he still felt a crushing emptiness inside him. Melancholy hung on him like a shroud.

Whatever had happened in that supermarket, for some reason he felt dimly responsible for it. He couldn't quite understand why he felt that way. After all, he had been nowhere near it when it happened.

But you should have been, a voice whispered angrily to him. *You should have been there. You never should have let yourself get braindrained. You were careless and clumsy, and because of that, people died.*

That was so unfair. He was as human as anyone. If someone took advantage of him, if someone caught him unawares and had reduced him to this amnesiac state, there was no way that he should take on the guilt for things that happened as a result. It was the fault of whoever had done it to him. They were responsible for the deaths in that supermarket. They were responsible for unleashing—

Images flashed before him. Huge, glistening teeth and a roar like a locomotive. Incredible ferocity that he barely managed to hold in check.

Not a care in the world.

What madness that seemed. Every muscle in his body felt careworn.

He was reacquiring a sense of what the life he had been leading had been like, and it was nothing that he was happy about. Once it might have been peaceful. But all he could think of now was several years of fear, of running, of a dread sense that *this was as good as it was going to get*. It was never going to get any better. He would be chased and hounded until he was caught or until he was dead. There would never be any respite or relief, and he would be watching over his shoulder for the rest of his life. Never able to relax. Never able to trust.

The concept of finding the place called Haven was a frightening one. He couldn't recall when he had first heard of it—that was lost in the haze of confusion that was his memory. But the moment that he had, he knew that it represented hope, salvation—a place where the running could end. A place filled with people like himself.

Now, finally, he had reason to believe that the mythical Haven was not far off. That it might literally be under his very nose. And faced with this, he found that he was frightened. What if . . . what if he had built himself up for nothing? What if he found Haven, and it wasn't the place of safety that he'd dreamed of? After all, just inquiring about it had lost him a precious part of himself.

What if he never reacquired whatever had left the vacancy in his soul?

He looked toward the sky, the constant, oppressive pollution-filled gray sky that had changed every single day into one laced with mourning. Mourning for a world gone wrong. Mourning for himself.

He sank down onto the sand, weariness pounding him down. He felt numb. He wasn't even sure if he wanted to get his memory back. The glimmerings he was able to discern only served to give him the feeling that the full measure of his memory might drive him completely over the edge. He had lost his memory, his home, his peace of mind; he had lost himself. How much loss was someone supposed to take before they were completely lost themselves? How much pressure did his back have to bend under before it broke?

He heard a soft *shuck-shuck* on the sand behind him. He knew who it was, but it didn't matter. Nothing mattered. He sank down onto the sand, removed his shoes, and allowed the cold, dirty water to swirl around his toes.

"You'll get sick from that," said Alex. "Come on."

"I don't want to," he said.

"Why?"

"I'm afraid of what I'll find."

He turned and faced her. She was looking up at him with annoyance, and then she saw what was in his face and her expression softened considerably. "Chuck," she said quietly. "It's okay. Really."

"What if I'm stuck like this?" he said. "What if I'm stuck feeling this way for the rest of my life, with this . . . nothingness inside me. I never thought that 'nothing' could hurt so much. I feel like . . . like instead of where I should be . . . there's just a hole. God"—and he looked skyward—"what if it really, truly never gets better. What if I can never get back what I was? Jesus, what if it gets worse? If you hadn't found me in that alleyway, I'd probably have lived out my life like that—fogged and confused. Barren. What if things go wrong and it happens again?"

"That's not going to happen," she said firmly. "I'm with you and I'm telling you, it's not going to happen. You've got me watching your back." She put her hands on his shoulders. "It's going to be fine. You just have to trust me."

"I don't even *know* you!" he said. "I don't know anything! My whole brain has . . . has checked out! Gone out of town. The only thing I know for certain is that I'm scared. I wasn't before. But I am now."

"Chuck—"

He was trembling beneath her touch. "Chuck," she said again, and she touched his face.

She had not planned it, and certainly he hadn't. But the next thing she knew, her mouth was pressed against his, and she couldn't tell for sure who had initiated it or who was happier that it was happening. They kissed greedily, grabbing at each other, and Alex hadn't felt this clumsy since she'd been a teenager in the backseat of a car. As for Chuck, he couldn't remember ever feeling this way, ever.

It was insane. Now was definitely not the time and not the place. But somehow that made it all the more desirable.

They went down into the dirty sand, pulling at each other's clothes, not caring about who might see or where they were. They were overwhelmed by the sense that it all soon might end, that they were about to hurl themselves into unknown danger that they might not survive—and even if they did, they were both pursued by forces that were unrelenting and would, sooner or later, destroy them. And even if, by some miracle, those pursuing forces were not able to bring them down, well, the world was poised on the brink of its demise. Ready to drown in the poisons that had been fed it by its children.

Nothing seemed to matter. Nothing except the pounding of their blood, the press of their skin against each other, the desperate need by both of them to feel *something* instead of fear and a drive for self-preservation.

They gave to each other now. Alexandra gasped, her fingers digging into his shoulders as she moved with him, and then running her hands along the length of his hardened body. Around them the air was chill coming in off the ocean, and the sand was cold and damp, but that didn't matter. None of it mattered except for the heat that pounded through them. The heat that grew and grew and exploded like a long pent-up volcano, and gave them, just for a few minutes, escape from the world. Respite from the unrelenting misery of their situation. Gave them, just for a few minutes, peace.

For long minutes after it was over they lay pressed against each other, unwilling to separate. Afraid to let the heat from their bodies dissipate into the uncaring and polluted air. Eventually, though, the awareness of where they were and the things they had to do—the rudeness of real world necessities—impinged on them to the point where they couldn't ignore it.

They stood and brushed the sand off each other's naked bodies, smiling sheepishly and feeling a little embarrassed and yet happy to be embarrassed. Happy to feel something besides numbing and constant dread.

"Uhhh . . . thanks," said Chuck at length as he pulled his clothes on.

"Hey, no problem," replied Alex, pulling her shirt on over her head. "I mean . . . you never know, right? You never know what could happen and—"

"Right."

They smiled at each other, again feeling slightly disconcerted, and then Chuck cleared his throat loudly as if this were a signal that they had to concentrate on matters that were at hand. He smiled briefly at the indentation in the sand that they had left as he said, "So . . . where do you think they are?"

She scanned the view from where they were. The boardwalk stretched along what had once been a thriving community of shops, arcades, and so on. Everything had been boarded and shut up. It was like a ghost town, and considering what they had just been up to moments ago, she was actually somewhat relieved. Visible in the distance on the edge of the boardwalk was the RAC 3000, waiting patiently. Alex wondered if the RAC had been able to detect what they'd been up to. She even wondered, oddly enough, if the car would be jealous. Worse—she seemed to view both Chuck ("Charles") and Alex ("Alexandra") and her (again "her"?! Why couldn't Alex think of the car as an "it"?) relationship with them as protective. Parent watching over errant children. So if they were her children and they had been humping on the beach, well . . . they were probably going to be getting an earful from her.

"Well." She licked her lips, trying not to think about that rather unpleasant likelihood. "We could go building to building. Break into each one, check out the interior. See what we find. Do it all at random. Or—"

"Or what?"

"Or we could do what I was going to tell you about before we . . . got distracted. Namely, follow the footprints I found."

"Footprints?"

She nodded briskly. "Under the boardwalk. Clinging to the edge of the wall, as if they were concerned about staying hidden."

"They? More than one person?"

"Not exactly. One person. One dog."

12

Mu lay stretched out on a table in one of the few still-functioning emergency rooms in the five boroughs. She was muttering a string of profanity, all of which fell on deaf ears to the doctor, who was studying X rays intently.

"You've got a mild concussion," he said at last. "We're going to have to keep you here for at least twenty-four hours for observation."

"Fuck you, magoo," she said, sitting up abruptly. But doing so was a big mistake, because the world spun around her and she hit the floor. She wretched once, but brought up nothing except a dribble of bile, which, the doctor thought bleakly as he helped her back onto the bed, probably was her natural sustenance anyway.

"Happy?" he said, trying to keep the smugness out of his voice. There was nothing in his Hippocratic Oath that said he had to like every patient he dealt with. And considering the vast number of scum who paraded through the doors of the clinic—for that was what seemed to be all that was left in New York these days—it was harder and harder to find anyone even tolerable.

"Look, Dr."—she glanced at his nametag—"Dr. R. Faber. I don't have time for this. I gotta get after the guy who did this to me."

He sighed inwardly, and wished for the umpteenth time that he had the brains or luck of his older brother, Martin. His brother was off somewhere involved in all sorts of exciting research into cybernetics, and here he was trapped in some crummy emergency room in Queens, dealing with psychotic obsessions like this one. "I'm afraid you're not going anywhere immediately. For one thing, you and your associates ride motorcycles. Well, you're going to find that your sense of balance is shot to hell. So the first time you try and ride, you're going to smear yourself all over the street. Secondly, you could die. Nurse," and he gestured to the nurse standing just behind him. She had only joined the staff a day or so ago, but that wasn't unusual. The turnover they had in this place was nothing short of phenomenal. He gestured toward the bleeding that was starting on Mu's forehead. The nurse nodded and stanched the bleeding with quick efficiency.

He checked the bleeding and said, "The first thing we have to do is sew that up. Nasty piece of work. Who did it to you?" Not that he really cared, but he wanted to say something to distract her from the proceedings.

"A guy who made me fly through the air, just by waving at me."

"Oh, really." He carefully kept his voice neutral.

"Yeah, really," she said. "It was like the air just

picked me up and tossed me around. And he had this cute piece of meat with him. And a car with an attitude."

"I see."

His very lack of skepticism was more than enough to let Mu know that he thought she was full of shit, or drugged up, or brain-damaged, or something. "You don't believe me."

"I believe you believe it," he said with a shrug, preparing the sutures. "More than that is irrelevant. Doesn't matter what I believe, does it?"

"No, it doesn't. Just get me fixed up so I can go after him."

"How do you know where he is?"

"Coney Island. He was muttering about Coney Island. And when I get out there . . . hey. Is it getting dark in here?"

And she passed out.

The doctor frowned and checked her pulse and respiration. Everything steady. The blow to her head had finally taken its toll, that was all. Something of a relief, really. Her yammering was unquestionably getting on his nerves. "Okay, Nurse," he said briskly. "Let's get her attended to, shall we?"

The procedure took no more than fifteen minutes, now that Mu's yammering was stilled. The doctor finished up with her, packed her off to a room, and then went out to do the thing he least looked forward to: Telling the half a dozen or so biker bitches in the waiting room that their fearless leader was going to have to stay put for at least a day, maybe longer.

The nurse, in the meantime, went quickly to a telephone and dialed a certain number that bounced off several relay stations before finally being picked up on the second ring.

"Yes," said the voice of Genady Korsakov.

"This is Petra," said the nurse. "I have some news for you . . ."

13

It was just as Alex had said. The footprints of a human beside the pawprints of a dog. Chuck immediately knew by the size of the prints that it was the same animal that had been in the supermarket. Somehow it didn't fill him with a sense of security.

Alex stepped next to the human footprint, measuring it against her own. "Smaller," she said, "and I don't exactly have big feet. Probably the young girl that our rather disoriented friend mentioned. Stealthy by nature."

"Why do you say that?"

She shrugged as if it were self-evident. "The depressions in the sand are at the balls of her feet, instead of being evenly distributed. She was tiptoeing, even though there was no reason to suspect that she was being watched."

"Maybe she was running," said Chuck. "Running people sometimes run on the balls of their feet."

"Distance is all wrong. If she were running or sprinting, the prints would be farther apart. Same thing with the dog, who's in a steady trot. No, they were proceeding at a pretty leisurely pace. Cautious, but leisurely."

They followed the prints, neither of them saying a word. There was a moment, though, when Alex's hand brushed against Chuck's and she allowed it to linger there for a moment. It brought a smile to his lips, and it was the first time in a while that he could recall genuinely smiling. It felt damned good.

The footprints ended at a heavy iron door, apparently rusted over. Alex studied it for a moment, and then turned to Chuck. "Okay. Do it."

He looked at her, puzzled. "It?"

"Get the door open."

He shrugged, reached for the door, and pulled. It didn't so much as budge. "Problem," he said.

"Shouldn't be for you," she replied. "Come on. Use your mind. Manipulate the lock, or just use brute force. Get it open."

She expected some sort of protest from him, some declaration that it was too hard, that he didn't know how to do it. But instead he simply nodded and took a step back, as if surveying the situation. Then he rubbed his temples as if trying to jumpstart his brain. His eyes narrowed, his concentration completely on the task in front of him.

Alex looked from Chuck to the door and back again. She wondered if she stepped in between Chuck and the door, what would happen to her? Would she be blocking a physical phenomenon that would cause her to be shaken apart? Or would she be utterly unharmed, since his concentration was on the door? Would that cause the power to go around her?

The door began to shudder and moan on its hinges, and then with a rending and snap of metal, it flew open.

She decided that it was probably better that she hadn't tried to find out.

"After you," he said.

"Oh, gee, thanks," she replied. "You're just too good to me."

One more time she offered him a gun, but he shook his head. She shrugged, stuck one in the back of her belt, and kept the other level in front of her. Chuck followed, watching their back.

They paused at the threshold, giving their eyes time to adjust to the dimness in front of them. A musty odor hung in the air as they slowly made their way through the corridor. Chuck fought down the impulse to sneeze, although he didn't see what difference it made. The ripping open of the door must have made some sort of sound, so whoever was inside probably knew that there were intruders. The only question that lay before them was how long before something was done about it.

Chuck suddenly stopped and glanced at the wall. He felt the hairs rising on the back of his neck. Realizing he was no longer following her, Alex came to a halt, glancing back at him. "Problem?" she asked.

"I think we're being watched," he said.

She licked her lips and nodded. "Okay. Okay, we're being watched. Nothing we can't handle. You and me. Team supreme."

"Right," he said.

And suddenly someone was blocking their way.

Chuck's face twisted in surprise and revulsion, but the more practiced Alex managed to keep a poker face. Even in the poor illumination, the features of the person—or whatever—who was in front of them were easy enough to discern.

"What the hell happened to you?" she asked.

Horny Toad made no reply, but his eyes seemed to swivel a bit in their sockets.

"You understand English?" she asked. When he made no reply, she asked similar questions in French, Russian, Japanese, Spanish, and even an obscure Cajun dialect she'd picked up during a stint in New Orleans. None of them seemed to penetrate.

"All right then," continued Alex, and she brought her gun level with his face. "How about this then. You do as I say, and I won't have to make your face any uglier than it already is."

Chuck put a cautioning hand on her shoulder. "Alex, take it easy. We *are* the intruders here, remember."

"Leave this to me, okay, Chuck?" she asked out of the corner of her mouth. "The thing you have to establish early on in any situation is who's the boss." She raised her voice and said, "Isn't that right, Chief?"

Horny Toad appeared to consider that for a moment. As he did so, he made a rolling motion with his mouth.

And then he spit.

The glob of expectoration sailed with remarkable accuracy and struck Alex's gun. Before she could even register disgust, she went straight to alarm. Her gun began to hiss and then melt in her hands, and she dropped it quickly. It didn't clatter to the floor so much as plop, because it was already becoming reduced to a small puddle of molten metal. Smoke hissed up from it as it bubbled, creating a small hole in the floor.

"You son of a bitch!" she said, and started to move for the gun that was concealed at the small of her back, but Chuck stopped her.

"I wouldn't," he said.

"He melted my gun! He spit acid and he melted my gun!"

"Did it occur to you that he could have melted your face?" asked Chuck. "He obviously hit what he was aiming at. Don't give him an excuse to take aim again."

They stood bolt still as Horny Toad studied them with open curiosity. And then, to Alex's surprise, he spoke. "This is not your place," he said, although with his gravelly, croaking voice it came out more, "This is nuh-AWWWWT YOOOOuur plaze."

"I want my dog," said Chuck firmly.

This actually seemed to register some surprise in Horny Toad's face. Then, cannily trying to cover, he said, "What dog?"

"German shepherd. Big as a horse. Nasty. 'Z' in his fur, on his head." He didn't think for a moment that this odd individual was unaware of what dog was under discussion, but he was determined to be polite.

"Haven't seen him."

"Yeah, right," said Alex contemptuously.

"Look," said Chuck, "we can go around in circles on this or not. It's up to you. But I'm getting my dog back, now." He raised his voice and shouted, "Rommel!"

Horny Toad suddenly rolled his cheeks around, and Alex shouted a warning just as he spit directly at Chuck's face.

The spit halted approximately five inches from Chuck's face. He took a step back and allowed it to fall harmlessly to the floor in front of him.

Horny Toad grunted in surprise, and then he croaked in alarm as he suddenly flew straight up. His head thudded against the ceiling and when he hit the floor again, he was unconscious.

"Nicely done," said Alex.

And suddenly Chuck felt extreme alarm buzzing through him. He looked up, and there was a very familiar figure. A figure that he should not have recognized, and yet immediately did.

"Him!" he shouted. "He's the one who did it to me! Who made me forget!"

Brainpan smiled his dark, forbidding smile, and from all around him now others were emerging. Both genders, a variety of ages, but all with a mixture of fear and defiance in their eyes.

And there was one girl in particular, who Chuck locked eyes with. A girl whom he instinctively knew had been the one who now had Rommel.

"I want my dog," he said icily.

"Get him," said Brainpan.

They charged forward on his command, and Chuck blasted out with his TK power. He didn't even give the others an opportunity to fully launch their attack as he lashed out quickly, efficiently, sending them reeling, buffeting them with wave upon wave of psionic power. Even Alex was impressed as Chuck's command over his abilities became stronger with each passing moment.

The attackers, meantime, had had no idea that the individual they were ganging up against had any sort of formidable powers. They shrieked in protest, as if angered that he should be allowed to do this to them.

Alex smiled, drawing confidence from Chuck's power. She hadn't even bothered to draw her gun. Chuck seemed to have matters well in hand.

Chuck felt various individuals trying to launch mental assaults against him. One was trying to influence him to go to sleep, another was trying to generate extreme heat around him. Given time, they could probably take him down. But he was not about to give them that time, and furthermore, their powers were like his in that they needed to be able to concentrate in order to use them. That was something he was not allowing.

He began to stride forward, step by unstoppable step, shoving them as a whole back, back. "I want my dog," he said again.

The girl tried to scramble away, and now Chuck separated a small portion of his mind and ordered her to come to him. With a yelp she was yanked backward through the air into Chuck's grasp. He spun her around, gripping her firmly by the shoulder, and said again, very slowly, very determinedly—all the while keeping the others at bay—"I want . . . my . . . *dog*."

And at that moment he heard a pounding, toenails clacking with staccato speed, and he looked up just in time to see Rommel, big as ever and twice as furious, leap through the air straight at Chuck. There was murder in the dog's infuriated face.

14

The Magistrate sat in his straight-backed chair, reading one of his books on the First Amendment. You couldn't find these books anymore—not since the Bill of Rights had been abolished. As a matter of fact, there were a lot of things you couldn't find anymore . . . except here. In Haven. Here, a man could command his own destiny. Here, there was free thought, accommodations, order, and justice. Always justice.

Then he looked up from his reading in puzzlement. There were the sounds of violence. Anger. Fury, here within Haven. He frowned. Such things were not permitted. If there were disputes, they were to be brought before the Magistrate. That was the law, under which everyone in Haven abided.

He rose, pulling his loose purple robes around him, and suddenly Oracle entered. Of all the Forsaken, she was the only one who came and went as she pleased, unannounced and unstopped. The Magistrate never remonstrated her for it. It would not have done any good. Oracle lived with her mind in a perpetual state of distraction as she looked toward the future. The niceties of living in the present day were lost on her.

She had long red hair that cascaded around her, and in keeping with her name, she was wearing a short, togalike dress and Roman sandals. She glanced around the room, as if searching for something that wasn't there, but might be in the near future, and then turned to the Magistrate. "The time has come that we spoke of."

He raised a white eyebrow. "The dog's owner has arrived?"

"Yes."

"What goes on?" He walked from around his desk. "Is he being welcomed into our domain?"

"No. He's under attack."

This stopped the Magistrate for only a moment. "Brainpan?" he asked.

"Yes. He would appear to be the leader."

"Do you know why?"

Her head turned, and she swatted at the empty air. She seemed puzzled, then turned back to the Magistrate. "Yes. Googie traded him sexual favors in return for his aid."

The Magistrate laughed low in his throat. "I am sure that's not the only incentive he required. He knows that all who have psionic abilities, and have business with the Forsaken, are to be brought to me first. He tests my authority, Oracle."

"Yes."

"Let's see how well he stands up to it, then. And let us check out this new psionic individual. If nothing else, my interest is piqued."

•   •   •

Chuck was momentarily stunned to see the teeth-filled behemoth leaping toward him, and entirely on reflex, he lunged to one side.

The dog shot past him, hit the ground, pivoted, and started back toward him all in a matter of a second.

"Get him, Zorro!" shouted Googie. "Get him!"

Chuck, from his crouched position, was on eye level with the huge German shepherd. He froze, staring into the monster's eyes, and then the dog charged him.

Alex waited for Chuck to dodge again, or even use his power to make the dog stop in his tracks. But he did neither. Instead, he offered no defense whatsoever, and the dog bowled into him. The two of them went down in a tangle of arms, legs, and forepaws.

Chuck's eyes never left the dog's, even as he buried his hands deep in the creature's neck and strained every muscle to prevent the snapping jaws from ripping his face off. The hot breath of the dog washed over him, the barking was overwhelming, deafening, and still he refused to unleash his power.

"Chuck!" shouted Alex, and her gun was out. "Rommel! Get off him!" She aimed the weapon, but the man and dog were wrestling around so furiously that she was unable to aim for fear of drilling Chuck.

Chuck sensed the connection with the dog, and knew that in that connection was a part of himself. And he was not going to be able to reestablish that link by tossing the dog around with TK power. But it was taking all his physical strength to keep the dog's snapping teeth from sinking into his skull. The animal's back legs raked down Chuck's, claws ripping his right pants leg and drawing blood down his calf.

With his physical strength diverted, with his mind

desperate and racing, pumped by adrenaline and not a
small measure of fear, Chuck's mind was spurred on.
The last of the barriers placed on it began to splinter and
break apart, and in a firm, decisive voice, buoyed by a
confidence that he thought he would never feel again,
he said, *"Rommel! Knock it off!"*

The dog came to a confused halt. He blinked several
times, as if he had heard something but had not been
sure of the source. Chuck immediately knew why, and
the knowledge gave him increased certainty in his own
ability. The dog was hearing Chuck's voice not just
through his ears, but inside his head. Whatever sort of
rapport he might have established with the girl, it had
not extended to the shared mind that he had with Chuck
Simon.

Googie looked at Brainpan in confusion. "What's
happening?" she demanded.

Brainpan gave no answer, except for some muttered
profanity. He had been certain that the boost he had
given his wipeout of the dog's memory would hold, and
under ordinary circumstances, it would have.

"Rommel," said Chuck with greater confidence than
ever. "Rommel, back off. Now. I mean it, Rommel," he
added. "Don't screw with me on this. It's me. Chuck."
And then, because he suspected the effect it would have,
he added, "Your master."

Just like that, the oppressive weight of the animal was
off Chuck. Rommel took several steps back, eyeing
Chuck up and down. His great head tilted slightly, as if
he were cogitating on what Chuck had just said.

And then a familiar voice sounded inside Chuck's
head.

Master, my hindquarters.

"That's more like it," said Chuck, grinning broadly. "Come here, Rommel." Rommel trotted over to him and then, pointing decisively, Chuck said, "Stay!"

Where else am I going to go, you asshole?

"Good dog," said Chuck serenely, not letting on the acerbic nature of the beast's responses. No need to let the world in on it. They wouldn't have understood. For that matter, he wasn't entirely sure he understood himself.

And just as he turned to face the people who had been attacking him, a hand clamped onto his forehead. Alex screamed a warning, but too late.

Brainpan leered at him, a cold fury in his eyes. And Chuck felt the sudden leap of panic that had seized him who-knew-how-long-ago when this determined and slightly demented psionic had last caught him unawares.

Rommel howled, directly affected because of the nature of his link with Chuck and the proximity of what was happening.

With an angry yell, Alex lunged to the side, determined to nail Brainpan right in his brain pan. And at that moment, Horny Toad came leaping in from behind, knocking her to the ground. The shot went wide and ricocheted harmlessly off the ceiling.

Chuck grabbed Brainpan by the forearm, trying to call upon his reflexes to save him. But his limbs were stiffening, and he felt himself balanced on the edge of a deep crevice. The darkness was beckoning to him, and in his mind's eye he could see long, dark tentacles reaching out to pull him down. "Get . . . your goddamn . . . meat hooks . . . off me . . ." he grated.

"Sweet nondreams, my dear Mr. Simon," said Brainpan, grinning.

And then a voice cut through the air. A voice of iron, a voice of experience, a voice that was clearly not going to put up with any shit.

And the voice said, "Enough."

The crowd parted like the Red Sea, and standing in the corridor, his hands at his sides, was a tall, white-haired man. And his left hand . . .

Chuck's eyes widened. The man's left hand was glowing.

"Enough, Francis," he said stiffly.

Brainpan's hand was still clamped on Chuck's head, but abruptly Chuck felt the pressure lessen. "I prefer 'Brainpan,' " said Brainpan stiffly.

"And I prefer obedience, and adherence to the laws," said the white-haired man. "Now release him."

Brainpan seemed to hesitate. Googie looked at him pleadingly.

The white-haired man's hand glowed brighter, and he pointed. A blast of white-hot power shot just to Chuck and Brainpan's left, frying the air around them, and an aroma of something burning reached Chuck's nostrils. Out of the corner of his eye, he saw a piece of the wall about three feet in circumference was now carbon-scored. Steam rose from it.

The hand was once again pointed, except this time it was aimed directly at Brainpan's head.

"This is it, Francis," said the white-haired man.

Brainpan released Chuck as if he had suddenly caught fire, and backed away several steps. Chuck's mind cleared immediately, and the moment it did, so did Rommel's. Rommel turned and started toward Brainpan, his growl filling the entire corridor. Nervously, Brainpan started to back up, and then Chuck said firmly, "Rommel, stop."

Rommel turned a baleful gaze at him. Whereas it had taken an achingly long time for Chuck to reassemble his memories, clearly Rommel had his act together much more quickly. It made sense. Rommel hadn't been on this earth for nearly as many years as Chuck, and besides, his life was much simpler. He defined the world in terms of things to be eaten, killed, defecated on, and humped. It was a no-nonsense world view that didn't leave room for a lot of subtleties, or even a lot of individual events that had tremendous consequences to him in the long run.

Chuck had discovered that Rommel's long-term memory of events, beyond sensory stimulus, was almost nonexistent. For example, Rommel remembered that they had met, but not precisely *how* they had met. He remembered their time in the circus in the sense that they had once been in a place that provided unique smells and sounds, and that he had—during their stay there—ripped the arm off that obnoxious man who kept coming after them. That the circus had been their home for several months, or that the man was Reuel Beutel, the Complex agent and psionic assassin who harbored a fear of dogs, was of little consequence to him.

Likewise, Rommel did not remember all the individual times when Chuck had, by the power of his mind, held Rommel in check when Rommel had wanted to kill someone or something. But he remembered that Chuck had done it, and he remembered that it was extremely annoying.

He tried to separate us, Rommel thought at him with unaccustomed ferocity. Rommel rarely let on that his relationship with Chuck meant anything beyond the concept that Chuck was a provider of food. *He tried to take you away from me. He got in our way. I want to kill him.*

"I know you want to kill him," Chuck said, emphasizing the last words very much for the benefit of Brainpan. He saw the brain drainer go ashen and turn to his fellows for some sort of support. But no one was making any sort of move. "But I said no. Clear? No."

With one final growl, Rommel backed up and took sulking refuge against a wall.

Chuck took a deep breath, and looked at Alex. To her surprise, he frowned. "We have to talk," he said in a voice that indicated that she wasn't going to look forward to it.

"As do we," said the white-haired man. He stepped forward and said, "I am the Magistrate, sir. Welcome to Haven. I think we have much to discuss."

15

It had been quite some time since the Psi-Man had broken out of the Complex stronghold in Virginia. Since then, all of the glass had been cleaned up, the buildings rebuilt, and a great deal of work done to rebuild it to what it once was. By and large, they had been successful.

And yet Quint still found it difficult to look out over the Complex from his office and not see, in his own mind, the devastation that had been caused by one man. Chuck Simon. The Psi-Man.

The reminder of that wreckage was ever-present, drawn crushingly to immediate memory every time he looked in the mirror.

Then his phone rang, and he picked it up. "Yes?"

There was a gulp at the other end, and then a voice said, "Tillis is dead."

He frowned a moment. "Who's this? Dini?"

"Yes, sir," said Dini. He was one of the field contact agents working on—

Oh, Christ. On the Beutel project.

It was with effort that he refocused on what Dini was saying. Something about having come in to relieve Tillis, and finding—

Quint made an abrupt slashing gesture, not that Dini could see him. "Beutel. Where's Beutel?"

"He escaped."

"Shit." It was rare that Quint muttered profanity, but when he did, it was because there was something serious going on. "Let me talk to Faber."

"He's dead, too, sir."

Quint's mouth moved for a moment before he was able to get any sound out. "Is there anyone else dead I should know about?"

"No, sir. Oh . . . a nurse."

"A nurse. I see. Thank you for bringing that up. When did this happen?"

"Just now . . . I mean, I just found out, sir." Dini was one of the younger agents, and didn't exactly have the hang of giving smooth, uncomplicated summations. "When I arrived at the hospital, it was crawling with local cops."

It was everything Quint could do to bite down his fury. "Goddammit, that's a private facility," he said. "What the hell do they think they're doing, interfering in this?"

"One of the civilian hospital staff found the . . . unpleasantness, and phoned the locals."

"I want that staff person fired immediately. Even civilians should know the rules better than that."

"Yes, sir. I immediately took charge on Complex authority. I believe that the attack occurred just a couple of hours ago, sir. I checked the parking lot, and I believe Beutel took Tillis's car."

"Just as well. Tillis will have no use for it."

"Sir—?"

"You're doing fine, Dini. I'll send backup there shortly. Keep the crime scene sealed. Keep those cops away from it. Shoot a few if you have to. I don't want any two-bit flatfoot forensics people crawling all over things before we can get our team out there."

It was utterly infuriating. The project should have been handled on the base. But Faber had insisted that he could only work in his own facility, and Faber was the best in the business. For the kind of work that Beutel was going to require, nothing but the best could possibly have done. He could have insisted, of course, that Faber do the work on the base, and Quint definitely had a way of being very persuasive. But he needed Faber cooperative, and he had been concerned that Faber might not have given his all, if forced into a situation. After all, it would have been so easy for Faber to allow Beutel to die and shrug it off as "one of those things."

So Quint had rolled dice and given the okay for the work to be done. And this had been the result.

Damn.

"All right," Quint said. "Thank you for reporting in, Dini. You handle things there, and we'll take it from here." He hung up before Dini could get out a "Yes, sir."

Quickly he dialed the tracer department. All of the vehicles that the Complex owned had built-in tracing devices. That way they could be located immediately, so that if an agent ran into trouble, then aid could be sent to the last-known location. It pissed Quint off that, relatively speaking, they had to deal with such primitive tools. He knew of those incredible computerized cars,

which would have been so valuable in terms of keeping
the Complex current with modern technology. But the
president, bless his heart, had been cutting back on their
budget and had declared that such high-tech vehicles
were beyond what he intended to allow the Complex to
spend. Quint chalked that one up to Terwilliger, too.

He ordered the trace department to punch up the specs
on Tillis's assigned car and get a reading as to its location. Within two minutes they had it pinned down as
being parked in a location approximately five miles
away from the Complex compound.

"Do you want us to send a squad to comb the area?"
asked the head of the trace department.

And that was when the gunfire started in the center
of the Compound.

Alarmed, Quint went to the window and looked out.
His eyes widened in disbelief.

Beutel, bold as brass and with a passing resemblance
to brass at that, was striding through the compound.
Both the military men who acted as perimeter guards
and a crew of Complex agents were firing upon him with
everything they had.

Because of the soundproofed windows, Quint only
heard the gunfire in the faintest manner. But he knew
that there on the ground the roar of the discharged ammunition was deafening. Agents and soldiers had their
RBG 40s and 50s out and were unloading on Beutel
point-blank. The fusillade wasn't even slowing him
down.

He charged through them like a fullback, plowing this
way and that, flattening them and literally running over
them. He thrived on the incredible physical ability that
this body—purchased with tax dollars—possessed. And

to make things even more murderous, he was clearly still in full possession of his psychic abilities. Faber hadn't been too certain whether that would be the case. He had thought brain damage might be present, or that the transition to the cyborg form he now sported might be traumatic to the degree that it would impair his ability to utilize his psionic skills.

Clearly that was not the case. Guns floated out of the hands of the attackers, spinning around and opening fire on those who had, only moments before, been doing the firing. Quint winced as Beutel massacred all who stood before him.

Even through the soundproofing, he imagined he could hear Beutel's demented laugh.

"This is not good," he said coolly.

At that moment the phone rang.

At first he ignored it, mesmerized by the sight of his people being slaughtered. The majority of them lay on the ground now, moaning or clutching damaged limbs or just plain dead. For a moment Beutel stopped, surveyed the destruction, and then angled back, looking straight up in Quint's direction. He shook a fist and started for the building that housed Quint's office. Quint contemplated having the elevator shut down, but what was the point? That would just delay matters. Beutel would simply walk up the steps. He would walk to the moon if he had to if it meant getting revenge.

The phone continued to ring insistently, and with a sigh Quint walked across the room to pick it up. "Yes?" he said.

To his surprise—but not too great a surprise—Genady Korsakov's voice came through. "Is this a secure line?" he asked.

"Yes," said Quint. "Look, Genady . . . this is not a good time."

"I sensed there was some sort of problem. Some sort of attack?"

"Some sort, yes. So unless this is really important . . ."

But Quint's ears perked up when Korsakov said, "I know where Simon is."

"You do?"

"Yes. You see, once we knew that Simon was in the New York area, we infiltrated some of our people into the emergency wards of the few hospital facilities still remaining in that charming metropolis."

"For God's sake, why?"

"Because our reasoning was that given the histories of both Simon and our own agent, with whom we believe he has joined forces, sooner or later they were going to wind up hospitalizing someone."

"And—?"

"And they did. And here's what we've learned . . ."

Reuel Beutel stepped off the elevator, feeling a bit surprised. He had been sure that some sort of action would be taken against him to stop him from getting to Quint, but none had been forthcoming. It was the damnedest thing. It was as if old Quint had just thrown up his hands in defeat and essentially said, "Come and get me." Not that any of that mattered to, or bothered, Beutel in the least. He would take Quint's head any way he could get it, but on a silver platter would certainly be acceptable.

He turned left and headed down the hallway toward Quint's office. Usually there were, out of routine, agents around acting as bodyguards. Beutel had expected that he would encounter them here, but was quite surprised when still no one turned up to give him a tussle. Now he was starting to get worried. The only thing he could guess was that Quint had lit out of there, in which case he'd have to start looking for him and that could take a long, long time. Quint might be a complete bastard, but he was also clever. If he decided to make himself disappear, Beutel would have the devil's own time tracking him down.

He got to the door of the office, and in frustration and uncertainty over what he would find, he kicked it open. Wood and the knob splintered off it, and he stood at the threshold and gaped in surprise.

There, surprisingly enough, was Quint. He was seated behind his desk, looking surprisingly chipper for a man who was shortly going to be swallowing his own entrails. Those chilling, icy eyes of his were locked on Beutel's and he tossed off a little wave. "Reuel," he said. "Here to test your mettle . . . or metal . . . I see."

At that moment, there was so much Beutel wanted to say. So many ways he wanted to express his fury and hatred of Quint. So many ways he wanted to let Quint know just how much Beutel appreciated being turned into a walking, talking sardine can. At this moment, though, no way seemed remotely as satisfying as just going up to the bastard and ripping him to shreds.

He forgot everything he was going to say and, with a roar, charged Quint.

And Quint held up a small box that looked like a remote control, and tapped a button.

Beutel felt his joints stiffen with absolutely no warning. His metal fingers were extended in a palsied manner, his legs locked up completely. He tried to focus his psionic power to yank the device from Quint's grasp, but it was as if his brain had short-circuited.

It had happened within a second. The next second, still carried by the momentum of his charge, Beutel fell forward like a massive tree. He hit the ground with a *claaaaanngggg* reminiscent of Big Ben.

"You . . . son of a bitch . . ." he managed to get out. So at least his ability to talk still functioned, to some degree.

He was staring at the top of the carpet, taking notice of dust bunnies, when Quint squatted down next to him. He was still holding the control device. "Looks like you've got a problem here, Reuel," he said.

"Son of a bitch . . ."

"You said that."

"Kill you . . ."

"Ah, but I can kill you first."

Beutel now saw Quint's thumb hovering over a red button that was below a black one. The black one must have short-circuited him. And the red one—

"Only two people in the world have devices like this," said Quint. "One you killed, apparently before he had a chance to use his. The other is me. And as you can see, I don't get caught unawares. The trick with the red one, you see, is that it will take the fusion generator that powers you and overload it. In about, oh, forty-five seconds, you'd be a cloud with an attitude."

"You'd . . . die too . . ."

"Oh, I didn't say I'd do it now," said Quint. "We'd take you to a deserted area—still paralyzed, of course—I would press the button, and be gone in a helicopter before you make your final departure. That's easily arranged, Reuel. And that would be such a shame . . . especially because it means that you'd lose out on your chance to even the score with the Psi-Man."

"Hate you . . ."

"Ah, but whom do you hate more?"

Beutel was silent at that.

"I think we both know the answer to that, Reuel. And if we can come to an understanding, why . . . I'll bring you to him. I'll set you loose on him. No holds barred, Reuel. I know where he is. What do you say?"

Reuel again was quiet, and then the small, visible mouth spread in a slow grin.

"Y'know, Quint," he said, "I always liked you."

16

The Magistrate walked around to the far side of his desk, pulled open a drawer, and faced Chuck, Alex, and Rommel. "I believe," he said, "that these items belong to you. I had Googie bring them to me.'"

"Googie?"

"The young lady who had taken possession of your dog. I assure you, by the way, that he wasn't abused in any manner."

"Oh, I don't think that Rommel would particularly stand around and let himself be abused."

"Ah yes, Rommel," said the Magistrate, sitting down and gesturing at the same time for them to do likewise. There were chairs set up directly opposite him, as if he had been expecting company. They sat obediently, something about the man commanding instant respect. Perhaps it was the fact that he had vaporized something with his left hand, and who knew what he could do with the right hand. "Curious name, that. How'd you come up with it?"

"The 'Z' in his head was like Zorro the fox. And he's

a German shepherd. And Rommel was a famous German called the Desert Fox."

"I see. Well . . . convoluted, but acceptable, I imagine. Here." He pulled several items out from the drawer. "A stack of Cards . . . false IDs, I would assume. And this rather oddly shaped spoon."

It was a spoon, bent into the shape of the letter "A," hanging on a chain. "Yeah, that's all mine, all right," said Chuck. He pocketed the Cards and placed the "A" around his neck. Alex was annoyed with herself that she hadn't noticed that it was missing. And for some bizarre reason, she further found herself annoyed that the "A" didn't stand for "Alex."

Chuck continued, "I bent it with my mind. One of the first times I used my TK power."

"Ah yes, your TK power. Quite formidable," said the Magistrate, steepling his fingers once again.

"You're no slouch yourself," observed Chuck. "I've got to admit, it makes me a little nervous sitting across from you, considering what you can do with a wave of your hand."

The Magistrate waved his hand and Chuck jumped slightly. If the Magistrate noticed the involuntary motion, he gave no indication of it. "It does have its advantages," he admitted. "Furthermore . . . but I'll show you."

He stood and backed away from the desk a few steps. "Come here."

Chuck looked at Alex, who shrugged. Then he got up and approached the Magistrate. Rommel gave a low warning growl, as if to let the Magistrate know that he was keeping an eye on things and no funny stuff had better be tried.

The Magistrate raised his right hand and held it up flat in front of him, palm facing Chuck. Chuck tried not to flinch. "Hit me," said the Magistrate calmly.

"I'd really rather not."

"Don't worry. You won't."

Chuck shrugged, drew his fist back, and sent a very halfhearted punch at the Magistrate's jaw.

His punch connected with air. Hardened, solidified air—or solidified *something*—that was in the air about six inches in front of the Magistrate.

"I'll be," murmured Chuck, and this time swung considerably harder. All he managed to get for his troubles were bruised knuckles. The air in front of the Magistrate held solid. "Some sort of shield."

"That's right," said the Magistrate. "A psionic shield. I can create it to completely surround myself, or if need be, I can instead project it to surround someone else . . . which can be especially handy if I want to restrain someone using less than fatal means. I solidify the air molecules, I believe."

He stepped away and sat down. Chuck pushed forward tentatively to see if his hand could now pass through and still he met with an obstruction. The Magistrate shrugged. "Usually takes a few seconds for it to dissipate, even when I'm not maintaining it. You should be able to pass through it now." And sure enough, the air was now clear as if nothing had ever been there.

The Magistrate held up both his hands, indicating his left and right hands, respectively, as he said, "My sword and my shield. With these, I keep the peace here in Haven. With these, I help to protect my people from outsiders . . . and, sometimes, from each other."

"This *is* Haven, then," said Chuck with a sigh.

"You've heard of us?" he asked with interest.

"A girl told me about it. Her name was Luta, out in Colorado."

"So word has spread," he said softly.

"She said"—and he drew his chair a little closer—"she said you were planning some sort of revolution."

Alex, who had yet to say a word, raised an eyebrow. Now this was certainly news.

The Magistrate smiled thinly. "That might be a rather extreme viewpoint," he said softly. "We dream of a time when things will be better. Actively planning a revolution, though? I don't think so."

"I say we revolt."

The half-dozen members of the Forsaken were grouped around Brainpan, who was crouched on the floor in his chambers with a look of fury burning in his eyes. Four Eyes cocked his head slightly and said, "Are you serious?"

"Damned straight I'm serious," said Brainpan. "After all, who died and put the Magistrate in charge?"

They looked at each other. Another of the Forsaken, a young man with huge ears that flapped about whenever he moved his head—thus picking up the sobriquet "Dumbo"—said, "But . . . he's always been in charge. Ever since I can remember."

"It's not like he was duly elected or anything. And it's not like we hold elections every few years to see if we still like having him about," said Brainpan.

"But he's always treated us fairly," said Fireballer, a young pyrokinetic who had once been a major league baseball pitcher before he had awoken one day and discovered that every time he swung his right hand in a pitching motion, a small fireball would emerge and lay waste to whatever it struck. Somehow the likelihood of finding a catcher who would receive his pitches seemed fairly remote.

"Oh, yeah?" said Brainpan. "What about Googie here?" And he gestured to her. "He took her dog away."

"But it was the other guy's dog," pointed out Four Eyes.

"Finders keepers," said Googie defiantly. "That's always been the rule so long as I've known. Oh, but not anymore. And now that guy has my beautiful Zorro. Did you hear what he called him? Rommel. What a disgusting name."

"So you want us to go up against the Magistrate because Googie's upset that she lost her dog," said Fireballer. "That right?"

"No one's asking you to 'go up' against anybody," said Brainpan reasonably. "Just let the Magistrate know that we think it's time for a change."

"And if *he* doesn't think it's time for a change?"

"Then," said Brainpan, his eyes glimmering, "we convince him."

And then he thought he noticed something out of the corner of his eye, but when he snapped his head around, it was gone. He shrugged and went back to laying out his philosophies to his audience.

"Where is this place, anyway?" said Chuck, gesturing to their surroundings. "How did it come together?"

"This place," replied the Magistrate, "came as a result of me. The structure itself is a block worth of abandoned buildings. A former bathhouse, an empty apartment building, a health club—there was an attempt to renovate along the boardwalk around the turn of the century that wasn't especially successful. The money ran out and then, some years later, so did the people who lived in the area. Ran out or died. This is not a nice place to live anymore."

"You have electricity."

"We have our own generator. It gets the job done."

Now Alex sat forward and spoke for the first time. "Who are you?"

He didn't look at her so much as in her general direction. "My name is Tom Jensen, although I don't have much call to use that name anymore. Around here I'm simply called the Magistrate."

She gasped in surprise. "Jensen?" she said in amazement. "Well . . . this is certainly an honor."

Chuck looked at her. "You know him?"

"He's CIA."

"What?"

"Central Intelligence Agency," said Jensen with a touch of amusement. "Back when there was a CIA. Back before all the intelligence agencies were absorbed by the Complex. I assume, from the fact that you know me, that you're an agent as well, miss." He tilted his head slightly, his eyes narrowing. "Russian?"

"How the hell did you know?" she asked in surprise.

"You do an extraordinary American accent," he said, "but there's just a slight nuance of Mother Russia in there. You should work on that."

"I'll try," she said.

"Do that, Miss . . . ?"

"Oh. Romanova. Alex Romanova."

"A pleasure, Miss Romanova. Mr. Simon, the lady is

quite correct. I was with the Central Intelligence Agency. I was one of their top agents, in fact. And then one day something very innocuous happened. My alarm clock went off early, and I pointed at it in frustration. And it vanished in a puff of energy—along with part of my bedroom wall. Ashes where the clock had been, and a large hole that cost a pretty penny to repair."

"It just . . . just happened one day?"

"Oh, not just out of the blue. I had been sick for some time before that. Extremely sick, as a matter of fact. And the doctors couldn't find anything wrong with me. I simply had a raging fever with no evident cause. Lasted for close to two weeks. I was flat on my back. In fact, a revolt in a small South American country failed because I wasn't there to coordinate efforts. I've always felt a bit guilty about that. And then, one day, just like that—the fever was gone. But in its place was my sword. In short order, I discovered my shield."

"Did you tell your superiors?"

"Oh, yes," he said softly. "I told them."

"And?"

"They tried to have me killed."

Chuck and Alex looked at each other, and then at him. *"Killed?"* said Chuck incredulously. "Why?"

"Oh, not at first," said Jensen, sounding worried that Chuck seemed so upset. "At first they wanted to use me as an assassin. Not that I'd never killed anyone, don't get me wrong, I had. When it was necessary in the line of duty, as part of some greater mission. But because I had developed such a devastating personal weapon—a weapon that could not be detected by any scanner, and could be used both offensively and defensively—I was tremendously desirable as a force for pure devastation. I didn't like the sound of that. It was not what I had signed on for. So I resigned. And was informed that resigning was not an option."

"So you left."

"So I left," said Jensen. "Went on the run. Led them on rather a merry chase."

"Why aren't they chasing you now?"

He allowed a small smile. On his grave face, it looked particularly bizarre. "They think I'm dead."

"How did you manage that?"

"Do you remember the nuclear power plant in Arizona that blew up about, oh, nine years ago?"

"Yes," said Chuck. "The one where about six people were killed."

Jensen uttered a short, sarcastic laugh. "Actually, it was somewhere around six hundred. Oh, yes," he said when he saw Chuck's amazed look. "Oh, yes indeed. The true devastation was covered up. The government has been known to do that from time to time."

"And they thought you were there."

"Oh, I was," said Jensen. "My personal shield protected me . . . but they couldn't know that. They had no idea just how durable it is. So when they were busy covering up the vast number of people who died, my name was simply added to the list. I became a nonperson. And that status was just fine with me.

"I wandered the country after that, and one by one I picked up followers. Oracle was the first, and her abilities led me to others. Haven back then was more of a concept than a reality. It was constantly mobile. Eventually, though, we settled here. And it became an even more desirable piece of real estate when Pittsburgh blew up, rendering much of this area unlivable. Indeed, if it weren't for the special air filters we have in the ventilation system, I doubt we could've survived here for the time that we have."

"Amazing," murmured Chuck.

"You are, of course, welcome to stay. Miss Romanova, we've never had a nonpsionic with us, but if Mr. Simon will vouch for you, I have no trouble with your staying."

She looked to Chuck and, to her surprise, saw hesitation flickering in him. Then he shrugged indifferently. "Yeah . . . sure. Why not."

How long are we supposed to sit around and listen to these boring discussions? demanded Rommel.

"Rommel's hungry. He likes fresh meat."

"He'll have to settle for canned around here," said the Magistrate a bit apologetically. "And dry dog food."

Get neutered. I'm out of here.

"You'll get used to it," said Chuck.

Jensen's gaze moved in momentary confusion from Chuck to Rommel, and then he seemed to shrug mentally. "I daresay he will. Now, Mr. Simon . . . I'd like you to bring me up to speed on your present situation."

The Magistrate leaned back in his chair and listened intently as Chuck told him everything that he could— about the first testing he had done that revealed both his intuitive and TK powers, his time with the Complex, his fugitive life since then, and the events that had led to him being an amnesiac in New York.

"I'd been doing some poking around," said Chuck. "Once I arrived in New York on the Bullet Train, I decided to hang around for a while, figuring that the Complex was still going to be concentrating their search for me on the West Coast. And I heard about this supposed gang in Coney Island—the Freaks, they were called."

"Yes," said Jensen, nodding his head slightly. "That's the nickname we've picked up in the streets."

"You were characterized as 'weirdos,' and there were rumors . . . rumors that wouldn't mean anything to someone who thought they were just listening to the rantings of burned-out druggies and hopheads. But to someone who had been keeping his ear to the ground for months, trying to track down a semimythical hotbed of psionic individuals, well . . . it was definitely worth checking out."

"And you got as far as—?"

"Ocean Avenue. That's when I got ambushed by the one with the strange eyes and the bad haircut."

"That would be Brainpan. Or Francis Beamer. He hates his name, so I use it when I'm in a particularly nasty mood."

"He was a cool customer, I'll give him that. Came on like he was a friend, and the next thing I know, I'm in the Bowery with the other derelicts."

"Apparently he took a fancy to your dog," said Jensen.

YOUR dog? said Rommel, bristling at the implied ownership.

Chuck let it pass. "I see."

"Thought Rommel there would make a nice present for Googie. Apparently it worked, but then it backfired.

Well, Mr. Simon, I appreciate your candor." He extended a hand, his shield hand. "Welcome to safety, Mr. Simon, Miss Romanova . . . and Rommel. Welcome to Haven."

17

"The end is coming."

The Magistrate looked up at Oracle, who was standing in the doorway of their sleeping chambers. "Pardon?" he said politely.

She walked to him and repeated softly, "The end is coming."

"Could you be more specific."

How odd, he thought, that he had the sick feeling he knew what she was talking about, but something inside him was making him prevaricate. Was making him act as if he had no clue as to her pronouncement.

"We are to be attacked," she said.

"We've been attacked before."

"Not like this. The forces of darkness are too strong, and will come in great numbers. And a steel warrior, who comes for the new one. For the Psi-Man."

"A steel warrior?" He raised an interested eyebrow. "How very intriguing. And what do you suggest we do?"

"There is nothing we can do at the moment. The Forsaken argue among themselves. There are some who feel that you should not be the leader anymore. They are not of one mind, and will have difficulty defending themselves."

"You augered that too, did you?"

"No." She actually smiled slightly. "Actually, Figurine told me. She was eavesdropping on the complaints of Brainpan."

"Ah. Brainpan. Now that does not surprise me at all. So . . . how best to proceed."

"Procedure does not matter. They will attack at sunrise."

He sighed. "So soon?"

"Yes."

He let out a long sigh and pulled off his judicial robe. He sank onto the bed, looking not at all like the imperious, confident figure he held himself out to be. He rubbed the bridge of his nose with his fingers.

"I am so tired," he said at last. "So tired of the fighting. So tired of it all. This country . . . it once was something so incredible, my love. You're a bit too young to remember. But I remember. I remember when we looked at other countries where free speech was rewarded with death; where human rights were trod upon beneath booted heels of dictators. I remember countries where burning oil wells turned the skies permanently gray, and entire populations sickened and died. All those things, and we seemed so lucky . . . so damned lucky . . . to be living in the United States. And now . . ." He shrugged. "Now it's all changed. It's all different. The government claimed they wanted to protect us. To save us from ourselves. And the Bill of Rights vanished without a trace. And the Cards came into vogue, making us into personality-less drones. We are watched. We are monitored. We are regulated, unto death. It's all just as was predicted in *1984*."

She frowned. "What was predicted in *1984*?"

"It was a book, by George Orwell."

"I never heard of it."

"Of course you didn't." He smiled mirthlessly. "You won't find it on any shelves. Not anymore. Along with quite a few other works as well. The government gets a bit nervous when it comes to things that make you think."

"Oh."

He rubbed his eyes. "Just so tired," he said. "Tired of not understanding why I have this power. Why any of us does. Tired of the burden. Tired of all the unanswered questions. Tired . . . and yet I can't sleep. All I want to do is sleep."

She went to him and sat down on the bed next to him. He looked at her beautiful eyes—the sightless eyes that looked blindly back at him—and said, "The best thing I've done in the last five years was marry you."

She smiled, remembering that glorious night. She had not been able to see it, of course. Her eyesight had vanished the same day that she had gotten her first precognitive vision. They had been deep in a forest when he had proposed. They had managed to find a waterfall that he claimed was over a hundred feet tall. She suspected that it wasn't much over ten, but hadn't let on.

They had stripped, stepped into the waterfall, and, with the water cascading down over them, given their vows to each other. They had not needed a priest, they reasoned, because a priest is simply supposed to be acting as an intermediary for God. Considering the incredible abilities they wielded, they were certain that God kept a permanent eye on them, and so anything they said to each other went straight to the source. In the sight of the god who had bestowed their odd, and perhaps even cursed, powers. Then they had consummated their marriage right there, in the waterfall, which Jensen had later pointed out was another terrific advantage over a church ceremony.

"The best thing," he repeated, and she smiled shyly. Then he was silent for a moment. "Is this our last night together?"

"I do not know."

She did. He could tell she did. But she wouldn't say. Her silence was enough to let him know, and yet he honored it.

He took his wife in his arms, and not knowing the future, he instead made love to the past.

And after that he slept.

There was a knock on Chuck's door. Rommel immediately lifted his head as Chuck half sat up in bed. Then Rommel turned toward Chuck and remarked, *It's her, isn't it?*

"Yeah, I think so."

And you want me to leave, right?

"It would be nice to have privacy for a few minutes. Don't worry, it won't take long."

Rommel rose and padded toward the door. "Come in," called Chuck, and Alexandra opened it just in time to step back as the huge German shepherd walked past. He gave her a disdainful glance as he did so.

"What?" he said without preamble.

She took a breath and let it out slowly. "I thought you'd want to know that I checked with Rac. She's parked in a small garage they have. Nothing fancy, of course, but it's better than her sitting out on the street."

"Good. Thanks for coming by." He rolled over and presented his back to her.

"Chuck," she said after a moment, "why are you being this way?"

"What way?"

"Why are you snubbing me?"

He turned back to face her, his eyes cold. "I don't like the kind of person you are."

She huffed slightly at that. "The kind of person I am saved your miserable hide. Remember? If it weren't for me, you'd be rotting away on the Bowery somewhere. Or have you forgotten that, along with all the other things you forgot."

"No I haven't," he said. "Of course, linking up with me served your own purposes quite nicely. Now you're nice and safe from the people who were out to get you. But instead let's talk about the things I remember. Like what you did in San Francisco. Like how you killed two innocent people."

She sighed. "I feel badly about that. You know that."

"Oh, I'm sure you do."

"Yes I do!" She bristled. "Look, let's just drop the holier-than-thou shit, okay, Chuck? I wanted to kill their son. I had to kill their son, and when push came to shove, I failed, and *you* killed their son. He was a monster, and they were the parents of monsters, so they weren't exactly innocent, but they weren't exactly guilty either. So they fell into the gray area and the gray area swallowed them. I'm sorry, okay? And I took their lives, and I've taken other people's lives in the line of duty, and I don't want to do it anymore. If I could give life back, I would. But I can't. Yes, I've done things I'm ashamed of, and so have you. The only difference is that you heap guilt and more guilt on yourself, and I just cope. Okay? I just go on with my life, because the bottom line is that they're dead, but I'm alive. And I'm not going to pretend I'm not alive."

His eyes went from cold to burning. "Is that what that was out on the beach? You wanting to be alive? Knowing how I feel about you, how the sight of you makes me angry, and yet you had no problem taking advantage of me on the beach."

"Taking *advantage* of you?" She laughed at that. "You sound like a teenage girl on prom night! 'Oh, Mother! He took advantage of me! There wasn't a thing I could do!' Give me a break, Chuck. Deep down, you must have wanted it, too. You sure weren't fighting me at all, because if you were, I'd've lost."

"I'm pleased you're taking my concerns so seriously."

"I'm taking them as seriously as they deserve to be taken. Look, Chuck . . . I think you're a hell of a guy. And you've got scruples up the wazoo, I acknowledge that. I didn't plan what happened on the beach. I don't even know if I particularly wanted to. All I know," she continued, and her voice dropped a bit, sounding almost tender, "all I know is that I wouldn't trade it for anything. Not even if it meant bringing back a life."

"Yeah, well . . . that's where we're different," said Chuck. "Because I would trade it. In a second."

He turned away from her again, and this time not all the coaxing in the world could get him to turn back to her. Finally she sighed and headed toward the door, where she stopped for a moment and turned back to him. "You saved my life back in 'Frisco," she said, "even after you knew what I was, and what I had done. And then you gave me the RAC 3000 to stay one step ahead of the people who wanted to kill me. If you find me such a hateful person, why did you do all that?"

"It's not something you'd understand," he said after a long pause.

"Oh, I understand," she said. "The problem is, you don't." And she walked out.

As soon as she did, Rommel walked in.

Did you hump her?

"No."

She wanted to.

"I don't care. There's more important things in life than sex."

Hmph, sniffed Rommel, before settling down to sleep. *And they call ME a dumb animal.*

18

The sun did not shine through the gray skies, but it was still barely discernible as being dawn.

Down the Brooklyn-Queens Expressway roared the Cycle Sluts. Riding in a sidecar, a helmet pulled over her head, was Mu. They had checked Mu out of the hospital on their own—at gunpoint.

Mu gripped the rails of the sidecar. She felt deep humiliation at this state of affairs, but that damned doctor had been right. She still felt a bit woozy after her earlier impact, and trying to ride a bike now would have been tantamount to suicide. Still, riding in a sidecar, like some sort of little kid—

Her girls weren't giving her any grief about it. Credit them with enough class not to rub it in. She appreciated that, no question. Almost as much as she appreciated the RBG 20 that was cradled in her lap, with six additional ammo clips attached to her belt. She cracked her knuckles and quipped, "Get something exciting between your legs."

Coney Island loomed in front of them.

• • •

Up from the south roared the helicarriers.

There were eight of them, each twenty men strong. Trained riot squads, the cream of the Complex crop. They had their weapons ready and were busy doing final checks.

But in the lead helicarrier, in addition to the twenty men, were two others. One was Quint. The second was the individual to whom the others were to defer.

The bare morning light glistened off Beutel's steel body. He grinned and turned to Quint. "Hell of a day, huh?" Quint merely nodded, keeping a wary eye on him. At the slightest wrong move, Quint was ready to push the button that would incapacitate Beutel and, if necessary, the other button that would blow him to kingdom come.

"So where'd you get this info? About Simon being in Coney Island?" asked Beutel.

"Informed sources," said Quint. And indeed he had. Not only did he have Korsakov's initial tip, but Genady had contacted him a second time, informing him that he had sent some of his own men—to be specific, the hit squad that Simon had thwarted earlier—into Coney Island, and after some checking and poking around they had turned up word that there was an entire group of psionics in hiding somewhere along the boardwalk.

It was incredible. A whole nest of them. Quint couldn't recall a time when he'd been so eager to go on a mission. At the same time, he was damned glad to have such a significant number of backups with him. Simon in and of himself was formidable enough. An entire crew—well, Quint would take what he could get. Those who resisted would have to be mowed down.

Those who would cooperate, well, they had possibilities.

No matter what happened, there was one thing that Quint was damned sure of. After Simon was disposed of one way or another—whether he was dead or whether he was incapacitated so that he could be brought back to the Complex and mind-altered—Quint was going to make sure that Beutel was just a smoky memory by the end of the day.

Seated in their car close to the long-shuttered New York Aquarium, the Russian agent named Gregori checked his watch. Krakoff was next to him. The other members of their crew were parked in other places nearby, trying to stake out the area in order to be ready for anything.

"Are you going to be having difficulty with this?" demanded Krakoff.

Gregori looked at him askance. "Now why should I?"

"I just wished to make sure. You hesitated before when it came to dealing with Romanova. I would hate to think that I have to report back to Korsakov that you are unreliable."

"I am not unreliable," snapped Gregori. "I am simply not a heartless killing machine like you."

"Thank you."

"It was not intended as a compliment."

"I know. That is why I appreciated it all the more."

Somewhere far, far away from what was about to occur, Genady Korsakov was sleeping soundly.

19

There was a pounding at the door of the judgment chamber of the Magistrate. He looked up from his book, closed it with a decisive thump, and steeled himself.

"Come," he said.

The door opened and Brainpan was standing there. Googie was at his right. Behind him milled a number of the Forsaken, about a dozen or so. Since the Forsaken numbered a little over forty, it was a sizable percentage.

Brainpan had a determined look on his face. "We're here to speak to you," he said.

"My door is open," gestured the Magistrate.

They filed in, looking amusingly to Jensen like children called into the principal's office. "Are you going to be spokesman, Francis?"

Brainpan was getting better at covering his annoyance whenever his given name was used. "I've been asked to speak on behalf of the Forsaken, yes."

"So speak," said the Magistrate. He gestured in Brainpan's direction and was even more amused to see that several people actually flinched.

Did they really think that he was that capricious? As leader, he had mediated quarrels, settled arguments. None had ever spoken against him. Everyone . . .

Feared him. Well, that was it, wasn't it? He was an aloof, fearful figure. He intimidated them all. Why should they feel any loyalty to him? Perhaps it was amazing that anyone had had any loyalty to him in the first place. Loyalty should be born of respect, even love—not fear.

None of this that went through his head was reflected in his expression. Instead, he simply gestured and said, "Well? I'm waiting."

"We feel," said Brainpan, glancing around to make sure that the others were still supporting him, "we feel—"

There was a low growl from the back of the crowd and the group parted immediately. Rommel strode in, looking like he owned the place. Directly behind him was Chuck, who glanced around. "Hi," he said. "I was just passing by, saw the meeting. Something I should know about?"

"We didn't invite you here, Simon," Googie told him. She looked at Rommel, unable to hide her feeling of being betrayed. Rommel, for his part, barely afforded her a glance.

"I didn't know an invitation was needed," he said.

"No, none is," the Magistrate said with an air of finality. "Go on, Brainpan. You were saying?"

Brainpan gave a little nod as if to reaffirm for himself that he was still in charge. "We feel that you have been running things single-handedly for far too long." He started ticking off grievances on his fingers. "We have no say in policy decisions. We have no say in how matters are run. There is no debate before you make a decision; you simply make it."

"You accuse me of being a leader," said the Magistrate. "Truly a heinous crime. One for which any judge or general or president would be convicted and hung."

"This isn't the army. Also, judges are appointed or elected. So are presidents."

"My," said the Magistrate, "you haven't been keeping up with political realities, have you."

"Our reality is this—we feel new leadership is required. You've been in charge for entirely too long. New blood is in order."

Brainpan then stood there, arms folded, having thrown down the gauntlet. He waited for the Magistrate to make a rebuttal.

Jensen stood up and walked around from behind his desk. He gestured to the seat behind it, the seat from which he had made so many pronouncements.

"All yours," he said.

Figurine had volunteered for guard duty this morning. It was a welcome opportunity to get away from the kitchen, and besides, she welcomed the cool ocean air against her skin.

The marvelous thing about sitting guard duty also was that it gave one a chance to catch up on one's reading. Especially when, like Figurine, one was so difficult to spot unless staring straight at her.

So there she was, her nose buried in an old science fiction book called *Vendetta*, when suddenly she looked up.

And saw them.

• • •

Brainpan blinked in confusion and glanced at his followers to make sure that they had heard the same thing. He looked back at the Magistrate. "What do you mean, 'all yours'?"

The Magistrate shrugged. "I'm no tyrant. I am in charge here because you people desire me to be in charge. If you feel that a change is to be made, then I shall step aside. I see no reason to discuss matters further, do you?"

Now others of the Forsaken were gathering at the door as well. Brainpan had spent much of the night trying to garner support from as many people as he could. The ones who were showing up now were the ones who had refused to join in, but were now extremely interested in the outcome.

Now the Magistrate turned and said, "Oh, I think you should know—"

"Ah hah!" cried out Brainpan, as if he'd just had some tremendous revelation. "Here it comes. I *knew* it. The catch."

"No catch," Jensen replied. "I just thought you should know that according to Oracle we're going to come under attack shortly. A devastating attack."

Chuck looked at him in shock and the Magistrate nodded, his eyes half-lidded. But from Brainpan there was only a rude noise of disdain. "Oh, now isn't that convenient timing," he sneered. "Threaten that there's some sort of danger in the offing, and wait for all of us to plead, 'Magistrate! Magistrate! Save us, please!' There is no way we're going to fall for that. Is there?"

There were nods and mutterings and affirmations of what Brainpan had said. Jensen surveyed the room and saw like minds. It was his own fault. He'd given them such a sense of security for so long that they felt invulnerable. Felt as if they were completely and totally safe.

He should never have named the damned place Haven.

The only one who displayed genuine concern for what Jensen had said was Chuck Simon. "Look," Chuck said. "If the Magistrate genuinely believes there's danger, we would be crazy to—"

"To listen to you," said Brainpan. "You're the one who shows up dragging the mundane woman with you. You're the one whom the Magistrate ruled in favor of for the dog. You and he, you're both pals. Why wouldn't you—"

And at that moment, Rommel stiffened. He growled, and suddenly Chuck felt it, too. Felt it with that strange sixth sense that always warned him of impending jeopardy.

"We're in trouble," he said.

The helicarrier was approaching the boardwalk, and one of the assault team was hanging half out the door, surveying the area with his infrared sniper scope. Suddenly he blinked in surprise. He lowered the scope, saw nothing, looked back through the scope, and damn, there it was again.

"Mr. Quint!" he shouted. "There's a naked invisible woman down there!"

Quint turned toward him. "Come again?" he said in surprise.

"A woman I'm not getting a visual track on, but I pick her up perfectly through the sniper scope."

"It's one of them," said Beutel. "One of the group you told me Simon hooked up with." There was a lot of the old excitement in his voice. It almost made Quint forget that he was speaking to someone more machine than man.

"She's running, sir."

"She's going to alert them," said Beutel warningly. "I wouldn't let her."

Nor was Quint about to. "Can you get her leg?"

"Yes, sir."

"Drop her."

Barely was the second syllable out of Quint's mouth before the agent had squeezed off a shot from his high-powered rifle. It cracked through the morning air, an ugly sound.

Dumbo was tilting his head back, those in the hallway outside the Magistrate's office backing up to give him room. His head was swiveling like a conning tower.

"Choppers," he said. "Five . . . no, six. Seven. Christ"—his eyes widened—"I think eight." And then he jumped back, as if he'd been struck. "Oh, God! Oh, God, they shot Figurine! I heard it! I heard her scream and—"

Instantly the Magistrate was out and running. Chuck was astounded how, for a big man, he was able to move so quickly. Chuck was right behind him and then was quickly passed by Rommel.

"Stay here!" shouted the Magistrate. "The rest of you, stay here!"

The sensors on the RAC 3000 suddenly started buzzing a furious warning. "Incoming attack squadrons," warned Rac, but there was no one to detect her call. And she was shuttered in the garage, unable to summon anyone.

This slowed her down for perhaps half a second. Then her engine roared to life and the car swerved around, tires screeching loudly within the huge garage. The door at the far end was closed. This didn't particularly matter to the RAC 3000, which shot forward like a bullet and smashed through the door without slowing down.

Figurine lay on the boardwalk, clutching at her injured thigh, moaning softly. Oddly, her blood came out perfectly visible red. She wondered why that was, and thought bleakly that she would never have the opportunity to find out.

The helicarriers were coming closer, stirring up the water beneath their blades. She tried to crawl toward the edge of the boardwalk and comparative safety, and then a shot cracked in front of her. It was a warning to stay where she was.

And then, suddenly, there were the sounds of heavy footsteps next to her, a familiar blur of purple accompanied by loud barking. She looked up through eyes narrowed with pain and a white-haired face looked down at her.

"Off to a rough day, eh?" asked the Magistrate, and then turned to face the helicarriers. Chuck was coming up right behind him, and Rommel was already there, snarling up at the incoming air vehicles.

"More of them!" announced the agent in the lead helicarrier. Quint and Beutel were busy checking out a high-powered camera scope that was now giving them a perfect picture of the boardwalk.

Beutel's eyes went wide. "There he is! There's

Simon! Goddamn, it's that son of a bitch! Shoot him! Shoot him!"

"Sir?" asked the agent, waiting for Quint's go ahead. But Quint was staring at the screen, for there was another man there who looked familiar. A white-haired man . . .

Beutel didn't wait. He grabbed the rifle out of the hands of the agent and shoved him aside. Leaning half out the door, he targeted Chuck Simon, said "Adios, Mother-fucker," and squeezed off three shots in rapid succession.

And just as he did, another man, dressed in purple, stepped in front of Simon and raised a hand. It shouldn't have made a difference. Those bullets could go through the side of a building—two men should have been as easy as one. Except . . .

None of the bullets hit the targets. They exploded, apparently prematurely, directly in front of them.

Beutel howled in frustration. "I had him dead to rights! I know it! What the hell—!"

But Quint had seen. He'd seen the white-haired man raise a hand, his right hand. Seen the bullets hit nothing and been brought to a stop. And then he saw the left hand being raised—

And he suddenly knew who and what they were facing.

"Veer off!" he yelled. "Veer off! It's Jensen! Jesus Christ, it's Jensen! Veer off now, goddammit, *now!*"

The lead helicarrier banked right so hard that they almost pitched into the ocean. The air crackled and burned just past them as a blast of incinerating psionic energy roared past them, air molecules exploding and making it seem as if they were caught in a mini-thunderstorm.

The helicarrier directly behind them exploded. It pitched over backward, its blades getting tangled with the props of the helicarrier directly behind it. There was the agonized screech of metal and the second craft went down into the ocean, crashing and burning.

And the oil that was so much a part of the ocean nowadays immediately caught fire, going up like a Roman candle. The men in the carrier that had survived the crash were dead within seconds from the flames. Wave upon wave of burning water pounded against the sand, like a beach in hell.

The beating of the six remaining helicarriers' blades immediately started hurling the fumes from the fire toward the boardwalk.

Chuck had picked up Figurine, trying to be careful of her wound but at the same time trying to figure out which way to go. "Behind me!" yelled the Magistrate, and Chuck and Rommel did as they were told.

Bullets rained down on them as Quint's helicarrier made a strafing run.

Jensen pivoted to track the angle of the copter, keeping his shield in front of them. "Stay close!" he shouted over the roar of the ammunition exploding in front of them.

"Can you make a shield all around us?" called out Chuck, concerned about being shot from the back.

"I can make one all around me or all around a single person. Otherwise my field isn't wide enough."

"Fire back at them!"

"I can't use my sword and shield at the same time," said Jensen as bullets continued to thud off their defense.

"Great! You got any other limitations I should know about?"

"Yes, I'm tone deaf. Now you get out of here while I cover your back."

Chuck glanced around, saw that the edge of the boardwalk was too far to make it without being hit, and then realized the obvious maneuver. He glanced down and hurled a bolt of psychic energy exactly one foot away from himself. The boardwalk blasted apart, and in seconds he had a decent-sized escape hole. "We're out of here!" he shouted.

Rommel jumped through first and right after that so did Chuck. He shouted for Jensen to join them . . .

And the boardwalk above him exploded in flames.

20

The Cycle Sluts roared down Stillwell Avenue in two rows, side by side. Then they heard the pounding sounds of the helicarriers nearby, the smell of burning air, and the explosions. Mu grew pale, suddenly realizing that it was entirely possible they were in over their heads.

At that moment, from the other direction on Stillwell roared the RAC 3000, Ultraflame model.

"Shit!" howled Mu. "It's the hell car! Don't try to take it on. Go on either side of it! That's it!"

The cyclists shot down Stillwell on either side, prepared to allow the RAC 3000 to go straight down the middle unharassed.

The RAC 3000, on the other hand, had different plans.

Within seconds of the approach, when there was no turning back, the doors on either side of the RAC flew open.

The car smashed right down the middle of the line, and the doors knocked the bikers off their vehicles with successive crashes and thuds. Mu, belted into the side-car, was the best served, but she was still damaged se-

verely as the motorcycle turned over and over before
smashing into a lamppost.

Now, although there were sounds of combat, Stillwell
Avenue was silent. The women lay about, broken and
bruised, unmoving.

Mu lay there for what seemed forever, and then she
heard a soft footfall. She managed to look up.

A bizarre face grinned down at her.

"Hi," said the Pezzhead. "You all must be here to be
our girlfriends."

Alex stepped out into chaos.

Everyone was running all about, screaming and shout-
ing and howling about the Magistrate. There was so
much noise, so much confusion, that she didn't know
where to look first.

Suddenly there was a massive explosion overhead, in
the roof of the building that housed the home of the
Forsaken. People shrieked in terror, and the whipping of
the air around them told Alex that hovering directly
overhead had to be some sort of air vehicle.

Dark forms started dropping down from the sky on
ropes and Alex backed up, reaching down and pulling
out the last gun she had with her, a snub-nosed revolver
that she'd secreted in a leg holster. She came up with it
just as the first of the attackers dropped to the ground
in front of her, and she fired once, nailing him between
the eyes. He staggered back and she would have loved
to grab his weapon, but more attackers were coming
down and she fell back, darting down the twisting corridors that the Forsaken had built, mazelike, into their
home.

●   ●   ●

The lead helicarrier landed on the beach, the roaring fire in the ocean sending off tons of black smoke into the sky. In front of them, the boardwalk was an inferno.

Beutel had leaped down first, followed by Quint and the others. He was whooping and hollering like a good ol' boy at a marshmallow roast. "Lookit that!" he yelled. "Isn't that beautiful! You nailed him! The guy with the hands! Told you the Naplaz would do the job! Goddamn, does that stuff do the job, doesn't it."

"I wouldn't bet that we got him," said Quint. "He's supposed to be dead, Jensen is. He was the most powerful psionic I ever encountered. Stronger than you and Simon put together. If he's still alive . . ."

"I wouldn't be concerned about that if I were you," said Beutel. "You won't have any problems at all."

"Oh, yeah? Why's that?"

Beutel held something up. Something rectangular. The remote control.

With a cry of alarm, Quint went for his gun. Beutel didn't have one. It didn't matter, because abruptly one of the agents who had been looking around for a target suddenly felt his gun wield around on its own. It fired one shot and Quint went down, clawing at his chest.

The agent looked in horror at Quint, not understanding what had happened. His comprehension was irrelevant, because Beutel caused the gun to reverse itself and shoot the agent as well. The others stood there in shock as Beutel strode off, in the direction of the offensive up ahead.

Their thermal readouts had detected a high concentration of body heat in the block of buildings up ahead that had been boarded over. It was there that Beutel was heading. It was there he expected to find the Psi-Man.

• • •

Chuck, carrying the injured Figurine, Rommel at his side, ran as fast as he could through the underground passage that led up to the main headquarters of the Forsaken.

He hadn't been able to see what had happened to the Magistrate. All he knew was that the boardwalk above him had gone up in flames, and that he had to get the hell out of there if Figurine had a prayer of surviving.

Suddenly he heard explosions from up ahead, and immediately realized what had happened. Someone was attacking from overhead. They were under assault from all sides.

He tried to turn and go back the way he had come, and suddenly Rommel snarled, *He's here.*

"Who's here?!" said Chuck in exasperation. Figurine moaned in his arms.

And then he felt it, too. Felt it and heard it, although what he heard didn't make any sense.

It was some sort of clanking, something that sounded like it was taking steps, like it was in no hurry. It was tracking Chuck and . . .

And it had a psionic trace to it. A trace that Chuck suddenly recognized, long seconds after Rommel already had.

"Beutel?" he whispered. "But he's dead. I saw him . . . saw him attached to the rocket. Nothing could have survived that . . ."

Then, around the corner, it came. The huge form of Reuel Beutel, silver and coils and pure mayhem from top to toe.

"Oh, my God," murmured Chuck, not believing his eyes.

It's him. His scent is all wrong, but it's him, Rommel said.

Beutel stood there a moment, ten yards away, and then he raised his arms and screamed, *"SSSSSIIIIIIIM-MONNNNN!"* Even above all the explosions and the distant screams, it was a bloodcurdling shout.

Chuck hated the concept of deadly force, was loath to use it. But here, confronted by a berserk robotic reincarnation of his most implacable foe—and with a girl bleeding to death in his arms—Chuck had no hesitation and no choice. He hurled a psionic bolt, a thing of beautiful lethalness, straight at Beutel's chest.

It slammed against him and staggered him slightly, but that was all.

Chuck sensed the problem the split instant he encountered it. Some sort of low-level generator, built right into the body, that scrambled incoming psychic force. In a direct attack, Chuck was helpless against him.

Beutel hadn't known. Indeed, no one was as surprised as he himself when he withstood the direct blast and suffered little harm other than being momentarily staggered. Then, with a roar, he charged.

Immediately switching tactics, Chuck blasted the ceiling in front of him. It caved in, pouring down on Beutel and burying him beneath.

"Come on!" Chuck shouted at Rommel. "That won't hold him!"

But—

"I said now!" insisted Chuck, and he turned and ran, even as Beutel began to dig his way out.

Alex almost ran into and shot Googie.

The premiere forager of the Forsaken was crouched

around a corner, her dart gun in her hand. It was trembling. When Alex came around the corner, she spun and aimed straight at Googie, who didn't make a move.

"Christ, I could've killed you!" said Alex, realizing at the last second who was there.

"I knew it was you," replied Googie. "I smelled you." She stood. "Come on."

Immediately she led the way, Alex being content to follow her. It was, after all, her turf.

They moved quickly, efficiently, and Googie always sensed when someone was ahead of them, friend or foe. It was tremendously efficient as far as Alex was concerned, and she was wishing that she could have such heightened senses when abruptly Googie had them at an exit door. She placed her face against it for a moment, concentrating, and then nodded and pushed it open.

They were outside, the smell of burning and cordite filling the air. Then they heard someone shout from overhead, "Down there!"

Directly above them was the helicarrier that had breached the top of the building. Roaring overhead were more of them, several angling down for a landing. One of the agents, one of the dark men, was standing on the roof of the building and had spotted them. He aimed his rifle at them, and it was far more powerful than the handgun that Alex was holding.

And then there was a sound, bottled thunder, the air splitting apart, and something struck the helicarrier dead center and blew it to pieces. A massive bolt of power that cut across the sky, incinerating the blades of the other helicarriers that were hovering nearby. Even the near misses were enough to blast them into the ocean. Within seconds, the attack force had been reduced to a total of one helicarrier, which was banking away to get to a safe distance.

And there, on the tracks of the elevated train, stood the Magistrate. His hand was crackling with energy and he hurled a bolt at the retreating helicarrier. But he had clearly diminished himself somewhat, for the bolt cleanly missed and the carrier managed to get far enough away that he couldn't harm it.

"Awright!" said Googie. "We're safe now."

The building itself was still crawling with dark men. Four Eyes ran from them, screaming, and Horny Toad leaped to defend him. The agents were under orders to try to take whomever they could alive, but if their lives were threatened, then they were authorized to use deadly force. Still, it was hard to envision the grotesque little individual in their path as dangerous . . .

That was, of course, until Horny Toad spit at them.

The glob struck one of the agents right in the face and he went down, screaming, his features running and melting into a ruined mass. The agent right behind him brought up his weapon and fired. Horny Toad, as agile as his namesake, dodged the bullet.

What he didn't know was that Oracle was directly behind him.

She never felt a thing.

Which could not be said of the agent who had shot and killed her. He felt a great deal when Horny Toad spit at his crotch. The Toad then put him out of his misery . . . but not too quickly.

And then he crouched down next to Oracle, and began to sob.

That was how Jensen found them.

• • •

Miraculously, Chuck found the same exit that Googie
had led Alex to, and when he emerged, Alex and Googie
were standing there trying to determine which was the
best way to go. Googie turned first, seeing him and not
believing it. Then Alex spotted him and cried out with
joy.

"Let's get the hell out of here!" said Chuck, and then
he suddenly realized . . .

"Zorro!" shouted Googie.

Rommel wasn't with him.

Chuck reached out and found him. He was back inside. He'd gone back for Beutel.

"Rommel, you idiot! Get out here!"

*He's mine. This will never end until he's dead, and
I'm going to kill him. And that's all.*

"Damn!" and he practically hurled Figurine into
Alex's arms. "Take her. Take her and get help, and get
out of here!" And without hesitation he turned and ran
back into Haven.

Alex took two steps, Googie helping her to support
Figurine, and that was as far as she got before the Russian agents caught up with her.

Jensen walked through the corridors, the limp body of
Oracle in his arms. He did not cry. He did not scream.
He was beyond feeling anything.

Beutel had cleared away the rubble and was now stalk-
ing forward, determined and furious. Suddenly one of
the psionics of the place, a young guy, was in his way.
He drew back his hand and hurled fireballs at Beutel,
which Beutel laughed at. He stalked forward, batted one

of the fireballs out of the way, and put his fist right through Fireballer.

He spun just in time to see Brainpan cringing against a wall. "Don't kill me," he whimpered. "Please . . ."

"All right," said Beutel. He reached out, gave Brainpan a bear hug that pinned his arms and broke every bone in his body. He left him behind, begging to be killed.

And then he saw the dog charging him.

"Yes!" roared Beutel. The old Beutel had been afraid of dogs, but not this Beutel. Not the new and improved Beutel.

Rommel lunged at him and clamped his jaws onto Beutel's leg. Beutel laughed and kicked him away, sending the dog flying against a wall. The blow momentarily stunned Rommel, and Beutel stalked forward, not even bothering with his psi power. He kicked Rommel fiercely and was rewarded with a loud yelp. It was glorious.

Rommel scampered back, tail between his legs, suddenly wondering if this was perhaps not the best of ideas he'd ever had. Beutel walked forward, swinging his massive arms in leisurely fashion. He grabbed a huge chunk off the wall and hurled it, causing the dog to duck away.

"Run!" he shouted. "Run, you bastard!"

And then Chuck Simon faced him.

Gregori had the drop on them, Krakoff at his side.

"Kill them," said Krakoff. "Kill them, or I will tell Korsakov precisely what sort of coward you are."

"Yeah, go ahead, Gregori," said Alex serenely. At this point, dying held no terror for her. "Shoot me. Shoot the young girl, too. And this one who's bleeding. Keep shooting and shooting and shooting. Makes no difference. Kill the whole world, why don't you?"

Gregori stood there a long moment and then angrily Krakoff said, "Screw you. I'll do it myself."

Which was exactly the moment that the RAC 3000 hurtled around the corner. It blew down the street and Krakoff whirled, squeezing off two pointless shots before being ground under its tires.

Alex leaped into the car, hurling Figurine into the backseat and ignoring Rac's protests that the upholstery was going to get blood-sotted. "All right, Gregori," she said as he stood there. "Now what?"

"You realize that if I try and take a shot at you, your car will kill me."

"Yes," said Alex. "But don't let that weigh into your decision."

He turned and walked away, leaving them to wait for Chuck and Rommel.

Chuck took a defensive aikido posture and waited for Beutel to come at him. He didn't have to wait long.

Beutel swung his steel arms and Chuck ducked under them, swinging his feet out in an endeavor to trip Beutel up. It didn't work. Instead Beutel shoved him with his feet and Chuck rolled back. He continued to do so as Beutel charged after him, his heavy feet shaking the ground beneath him.

Chuck scrambled to his feet and got tagged with a vicious right from Beutel that seemed to move faster than light. He stumbled back, cracking his head on the wall.

"Oh, man, I've been waiting for this," said Beutel as he charged the dazed Chuck. Chuck looked up just in time to see the bottom of Beutel's metal foot stepping right toward his face. He reached up, grabbed it with his hands, and twisted with all his strength, pushing his own body off the ground with his psionic power.

The sudden move managed to catch Beutel off balance and he fell, steel body crashing to the floor like a massive tree. Instantly Chuck was atop him, desperate, furious, unbelieving that this guy just kept coming back and back and back for more.

He slammed a fist into Beutel's face and was rewarded with bruised and bleeding knuckles. Punches were not his specialty. And Beutel suddenly stood, throwing Chuck off himself and grabbing him by the ankle before the Psi-Man could right himself.

Chuck saw the world whiz past him and then he slammed into a wall. Then Rommel charged once again, roaring and snapping. He ran straight up Chuck's back, using him as a bridge, and up Beutel's arm, and clamped his great jaws directly over Beutel's head.

Beutel screamed, the scream echoing inside the dog, and he dropped Chuck as he turned his attention to Rommel. He pried the animal off himself, gripping the German shepherd's jaws in either hand.

"Make a wish, Chuckie," he grunted to Simon.

And Chuck unleashed the full measure of his psionic power. It was not that he had been holding back. He had just never been quite this driven before.

Beutel staggered back, dropping Rommel, barely weathering the storm, and his robot body trembled under the barrage. A massive dent appeared in his right side, and had it not been for the generator, Chuck would have bent him in half.

"They wanted an assassin!" screamed Chuck. "Fine!

That's what they get! And there's not enough room for the two of us!"

And Rommel fell back, intimidated himself by the fury of Chuck.

And Chuck felt Rommel's fear, and Rommel's terror . . . *of him*. And Chuck thought, *Oh, God, is this what I've come to*.

For a moment it shook his concentration and Beutel felt the pressure relieved from his body.

Beutel used that moment to grip the ground in front of him and, with the added push of his psi power, ripped up the tunnel floor right beneath Chuck's feet.

Chuck fell wrong, landing on his elbows, and pain shot through his arms. He groaned and Beutel loomed over him.

"Hey, Beutel."

Beutel turned at the voice, and the last thing he saw was Quint, leaning against a wall, his chest covered with blood, a gun in his hand.

Then the world went white as Quint shot him in the eye.

Beutel fell back, blood pouring from his face, and Quint took a step forward and saw Chuck lying there. Then he took another step and fell flat. But he was holding a commlink device and he murmured into it, "Simon's here all right. I'm ten feet away from him. He—" Then he coughed, and blood came up.

Chuck started to pull himself from the rubble, and then he heard a low chuckle.

Beutel was holding something in front of himself. Some sort of little control box. And he pressed the red button.

• • •

The RAC 3000's sensors went into overload.

"Extreme heat buildup!" she informed Alex. "Estimate enough explosive capacity to destroy five square blocks. Estimate time of detonation—thirty-five seconds."

"Shit!" yelled Alex. She slammed the door and shouted, "Get us out of here!"

"But Chuck . . . and Zorro and Brainpan . . ." wailed Googie.

"I said out of here! Now!"

The RAC 3000 screeched out and took off at top speed.

"Failsafe device," murmured Quint into the commlink. "Beutel just triggered it . . . clear area . . . blow in a few seconds . . . Simon and I . . . both dead . . ." And then he stopped talking. His chest made an odd whistling noise and then stopped.

Chuck shoved the rock off his feet, grabbing Rommel by the neck and holding him close. He heard a high-pitched whine reaching a crescendo and knew that this was it.

Rommel licked his face. It was the first time.

"Good-bye, Psi-Man," said a voice from behind him.

His head snapped around, and he saw Tom Jensen, the Magistrate, his left arm around the body of Oracle. The Magistrate made his final decision.

He reached out with his right hand . . .

And the world went red.

Epilogue

The forests of Maine were one of the few places that
were still lovely, especially when autumn was just turning into winter.

Alex stared out the cabin window, waiting for Googie
to return from shopping. Figurine, who walked with a
limp these days but otherwise seemed fine, busied herself around the kitchen.

Alex gazed out the window and watched the leaves
falling from the trees, and wondered, not for the first
time, about Chuck Simon and Rommel.

She had, through her sources, managed to keep herself
apprised of the current Complex status of the Psi-Man
case, namely that it was closed. Quint's death had left
the Complex without a firm leader, and there had been
a great deal of political infighting about who should head
the organization. Finally Terwilliger himself had taken
the reins, and no one knew where that was going to lead.

Chuck Simon, though, was one thing upon which

everyone could agree. He was dead. No one could have survived that explosion. No one.

•   •   •

"Here's fine."

The driver of the pickup truck pulled over and let the red-haired man out the passenger side. "You sure, son?" he asked. "I'm going all the way to Paducah."

"No, this'll be fine," said Chuck. "Come on, boy," and he clapped his hands as Rommel hopped out of the back.

He had caught a glimpse of a Help Wanted sign in the front of a restaurant, and this town had looked as decent as any. Reminded him a bit of LeQuier. He started toward the door, Rommel by his side.

I'm hungry, Rommel told him.

"I'm going to get a job in this restaurant," Chuck replied. "And that way there'll be plenty of scraps and things for you."

Scraps. Great. Ever since I licked you, you take me for granted.

Chuck laughed softly at that, but it made him think of Jensen. Jensen, who chose to cast a protective sphere around Chuck and Rommel rather than himself. The sphere had taken the brunt of the explosion. When it dissipated moments later, it had still left Chuck and Rommel in the middle of a blazing hellhole . . . but that kind of escape was becoming old hat for them. He hadn't even been able to make out Jensen's corpse, but he knew that it was there. And he hoped that the Magistrate had gone to a higher court.

And he thought, briefly, of Alex. Very briefly, lingering almost involuntarily on their one night on the beach. And then put her out of his mind as he headed into the restaurant to introduce himself as Chuck Banner.

•   •   •

Alex stood at the window and saw the RAC 3000 rolling up the road. "Googie's back," she said.

"Good," said Figurine. "Hope she did a nice job shopping. You gotta keep your strength up, you know."

"Don't fuss over me," said Alex. Nevertheless, it felt nice.

She rested a hand on her stomach. She was just beginning to show. She wondered what it would feel like the first time it kicked, which should be soon.

"Could you get me the salt?" said Figurine, standing over the boiling water.

Alex walked over to the table and reached for the shaker.

Before she could touch it, it moved.

She stood there for a moment, her hand over where the salt shaker had been. She put her other hand on her stomach, shook her head reproachfully, and then picked up the shaker and handed it to Figurine.

"Wait'll you see what I've got in the oven," said Figurine proudly.

"That's nothing," replied Alex, "compared to what I've got."